A JOLLY LITTLE MURDER

A VIOLET CARLYLE HISTORICAL MYSTERY

BETH BYERS

For my Family

SUMMARY

December 1925

Violet Wakefield is determined to dive into the holiday and enjoy every occasion. She's going to see the live nativity, listen to Handel's Messiah, and attend the Nutcracker ballet. She'll cover her house in all the holly and lights. In fact, Vi wants nothing more than to put up the largest Christmas tree she can locate and stuff it with gifts.

She little expects, however, to stumble across a crime in action. When she gets pulled into the madness, her biggest concern isn't the crime, it's keeping Jack from committing a holiday homicide.

CHAPTER 1

*V*iolet leaned against Jack's bad arm. It was past the point of hurting him when she leaned in, and she wasn't sure she felt more grateful about anything. The scar was ugly, but he was going to be fine. Though perhaps not as fine as the dancers kicking their way through the Russian dance of the ballet. She tangled their fingers together. She needed to remember to tell Jack she wanted a record of the Nutcracker Ballet if he could find one. She had forgotten how very much she loved the music. It would be delightful to put on a record in her office and listen while she wrote.

During the standing ovation, she leaned towards Jack again, pushing up on her toes to say, "I'd like a gramophone for my office and the ballet recording."

He lifted an eyebrow. "Does that mean I don't have to buy rubies?"

Violet grinned wickedly. "The rubies are for getting shot."

"You know you want to leave early for the country house. When am I supposed to go last minute shopping for you?"

"Send a man. Make a telephone call." Violet's wicked smirk was a dare to make it happen.

Jack pressed a kiss on her forehead and then glanced at Victor and Kate who were on the other side of Vi in the box. "Shall we go?"

"Go get drinks?" Kate demanded, glancing between them. "Because I need some after all those weeks with my mother."

"I need some," Victor agreed, "after all those weeks without you."

"You mean," Kate shot back, "when you drove off to London with Violet and got into trouble?"

"Trouble?" Victor gasped. He put his hand over his chest and staggered before grinning at Kate and holding out his arm. "Shall we see if the bar here is still serving or shall we go find a gin joint with a band?"

"The latter," Violet declared. "I'm in full Christmas mode and want eggnog."

"Eggnog, a Tom and Jerry, or something with coffee, cream, anything to get me right zozzled," Victor agreed.

Jack shook his head and then said, "The Messiah yesterday, the ballet today, the train tomorrow. We're supposed to be on the early one."

"So, we'll go on the late one," Victor shot back. "We promised Vi and Kate full-Christmas with all the trimmings."

"The children," Kate said, raising an imaginary glass. "It'll be so fun with them."

"Father Christmas," Violet added, "with sleigh, stockings, and gifts. I can't wait to start."

"Rum cocktails," Victor said, saluting with his own imaginary glass. "Eggnog, mulled wine."

"Mmm," Jack agreed. He didn't sound excited, but Violet knew he was. They both loved the holidays and a holiday in the country with the large tree and all the trimmings? It was just what they needed after a hard year. Especially given how clingy Violet had been after Jack was shot.

Jack used his bulk to lead the way through the remainder of the crowd, Violet's hand in his own. Kate followed in the wake they left and Victor brought up the rear. It was Victor's auto they looked for with his driver at the ready and Violet wasn't listening when they named a club. She didn't care where they went so long as she got to dance with Jack, have a drink or two, and then head home only to pack up the dogs, the trunks, the book she and Victor were writing, and escape London.

They hadn't been back to the country house since she and Victor were called to London by their stepmother. Violet didn't think they even needed to stay in the country. She'd bought tickets for them all for their presents. The only person she'd given a heads-up to was Ham who needed to schedule time off of work.

They were going back to the Amalfi Coast, to the villa Violet inherited. They were going to bake in what sun they could find, sail the seas, drink the cocktails, sleep more than usual, and only come home when everyone had lost the bags under their eyes and remembered how to laugh.

"Gerald!" Violet called before he could escape her. "Wait!"

"Violet," her older brother snapped. "I swear if you don't let me leave, I'm going to lose my mind."

"Your mind?" she gasped mockingly. "However will we

notice?"

Gerald's betrothed, Lottie, laughed. "Oh Gerald, it's like you ask for her to tease you."

"Tease me?" Gerald groaned. "Violet," he said with exaggerated patience, "I will get your ward, I will tell Geoffrey you wish he could come for Christmas, I will make sure he understands that you love him, I will give him your gift, I will make sure that Ginny is warm and doesn't need anything for a few hours on a train where she has her own pin money and can look after herself. Especially since I have never met a more capable or independent young woman. Truth be told, I should ask her to look after me for the journey. Surely, I will lose my hat, scarf, or pocketbook."

"Surely," Violet immediately agreed, "you're right. Give Ginny all those messages and ask her to look after you for me."

Gerald groaned, Violet patted his cheek condescendingly, kissed Lottie on the cheek, and then wickedly handed over a wriggling basket with two puppies inside. Her own pups were claimed by others before Lottie came into the picture, so Violet had tracked down the pug that Lottie coveted and got her two. The wicked grin and evil wink were for her brother who'd be looking after the pups, taking them to potty off the train, and dealing with the worst of traveling with two pups.

"Happy Christmas, Lottie," Violet said, "from Jack, Victor, Kate and I."

She squealed as she saw the puppies and Gerald shot Violet a horrified look. Her evil grinned morphed into a glee-filled mocking expression that Lottie didn't notice. His expression promised revenge. Hers dared him to try.

Gerald sighed as he glanced down at the kneeling Lottie

accepting kisses from the two dogs.

"Thank you, thank you, thank you," Lottie cried.

Gerald couldn't help but smile at the look of his beloved being kissed sideways by the two little wriggling pug puppies.

"You're welcome," Victor said from the stairs, "you're welcome, you're welcome." To Gerald, Victor held out his hand and said, "You're especially welcome."

Lottie didn't realize the headache ahead yet, so she glanced up in surprise. Both men grinned at her, though perhaps Gerald's was a bit anemic, and then Lottie was distracted by another wriggled kiss.

"There's a lad there," Victor told Lottie, "and a lady. Different lines to keep any results healthy enough."

Lottie nodded, eyes shining. "My sisters will be so excited when their turn for a pup comes. Though perhaps Father would wish otherwise."

"I'm a believer in springing them on a fellow," Violet said innocently. Her wide bright eyes sold the innocent tone, and she handed Gerald the rest of the present of two collars, two leashes, a blanket for the dogs to sleep in, and some extra cleaning cloths. She saw him dig through, note the cloths, and shoot her another daggered glance. She was, however, impervious to such assaults.

"I can't believe you got me puppies!" Lottie was still beside herself with joy.

"They're good for the soul," Violet told her. "And my Rouge's pups have homes. Besides, we can't be tripping over only spaniels. I love the squished little faces of these folks." She scooped up the lad, nuzzled his nose, accepted kisses on her chin, and handed him to Gerald.

Her brother fumbled a bit with the pup. "I've always liked

bigger dogs," Gerald said. "But I suppose his face is charming."

"They're not for you, silly," Violet told him mockingly. "They're companions for your soon-to-be wife. They'll follow her around, worship her presence, and bring her endless joy."

"Oh!" Lottie said, suddenly blushing deeply. "Violet, I was wondering if I might speak to you alone for a few minutes before Gerald and I go."

Gerald bit back another long-suffering sigh that he would certainly let out the second Violet and Lottie were out of the way. With another mischievous grin, Violet handed the second pup to Gerald.

"I suspect," Violet told Victor, "that Gerald needs a drink before the train."

"Maybe two," Gerald agreed, shooting Violet another look of frustration. "I'm not sure why we even have to go get Geoffrey and Ginny. They've come home on the train by themselves before."

"Because," Violet shot back, knowing she'd partially pushed for it because of the puppies, "we're wrapping Geoffrey up in love until he's secure in our affections again. What a wonderful surprise to have his favorite brother escort him home and then take Ginny to us. Make sure he knows we wanted him with us, but Lady Eleanor refused."

Gerald had realized Violet's other intentions already and objecting just made him look like a beast in front of Lottie, so he let them disappear up the stairs to Violet's boudoir. It was a dragon-themed room in deep purple that housed her desk, her typewriter, the bulk of her wardrobe and a never used bed, since she slept on Jack's chest every night or tended to not sleep at all.

Lottie continued to blush until Violet found herself blushing along with the girl. "Is this about the bedroom?"

The red on Lottie's face intensified to a point that was uncomfortable to witness.

Violet knew she was blushing alongside, but she dared to grind out. "The act or..."

"The ahh..."

Violet nodded and crossed to her window seat, opening the compartment and pulling out a book. She handed over Wise Parenthood and said, "I hate that I blush when talking about this. We should be able to address it without feeling dirty, but here we are. I'll get myself another copy. You can have this one. It's a manual on birth control. If you and Gerald want to wait a bit—well, so do Jack and I."

Lottie didn't answer verbally. Her blush was so intense that Violet suspected she'd have trouble forming words. Violet took Lottie's face between her hands, kissed each cheek, and said, "I'm so glad we're going to be sisters."

Violet crossed to the mini-bar that Victor set up after one of their late night writing sessions went poorly. There wasn't any ice or any of the things that Violet preferred, but there was a good ginger wine which was her favorite for times like these. Violet struggled to open the bottle and then poured them both a glass.

Lottie took it with shaking hands and Violet shook her head internally. Externally, Violet smiled softly. She'd been older than Lottie when she'd married and had many a frank conversation with both Kate and Lila. She hadn't blushed nearly so deeply with either. But of course, Aunt Agatha had taken Violet for a drive in the auto and explained the works when she'd been far younger. The later conversations had been easier. It was possible, in fact, that Lottie's own embarrassment was making Violet remember that first discussion with Aunt Agatha rather than the later ones with her friends.

She realized that a similar conversation needed to happen with Ginny. Heavens, Violet thought, feeling her stomach turn. Heavens above. How did you go about having that conversation with someone you protected and loved?

How did you tell them that you would suggest that they wait until marriage to make love when everyone knew that Victor and Kate hadn't? Let alone Lila and Denny. Or Isolde and Tomas. Perhaps Violet was terribly old-fashioned? If so, what she somehow had to find the words to say was that it should happen with someone who loved and adored you. Especially that first time.

In saying that, however, knowing that Geoffrey and Ginny might well be in love—was she giving her schoolgirl ward vague permission to have sex? Violet took a large swallow of her wine and realized she'd already drained her glass. She poured herself another, eyeing Lottie. If Lottie and Gerald ended 'in trouble' it would be fine. They'd marry earlier or have an early baby and then be all right.

But what about Geoffrey and Ginny? Oh bloody, bloody, hell, Violet thought. She hadn't realized how hard raising Ginny would be when Ginny's grandmother asked Violet to take the child on and see her safe and healthy.

Violet pressed her hands to her own heated face and wondered if Aunt Agatha had explained nature, the results of certain acts, and her own advice half-zozzled? Because Violet suspected she might be drowning in her cups by the time she had the courage to speak. It was either zozzled or stuttering. Giving advice she had no idea was the right advice. She sighed deeply and then shooed Lottie down to Gerald before Violet went into a full-panic mode.

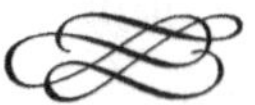

iolet tucked her head against Jack's arm and asked, "Do you love this auto more than the other?"

"The other is dead to me," Jack told her dryly as he stopped the machine just outside the pub. Their country house was near a village, but it was a good fifteen minutes by auto away from the house. They'd been discussing a good bowl of stew for the last hour of the journey and had decided to stop for food before they bothered with the house.

"What do you believe the villagers will think when we arrive?" Violet asked idly. "Do they look forward to your father arriving?"

"I can't imagine anyone cares what we do," Jack said seriously. His expression was surprised and he looked at her sideways as if trying to hold back a harsher reaction. "Did you think they did? Perhaps my father. He has friends here and keeps in contact. He even came down early to hunt with one of his local cronies."

Violet shook her head, scoffing. "I was just thinking about the differences between the people we know when they arrive into the home village and when we do. Like when we arrived in Denny's hometown. He knew everyone. I don't know everyone. What about you?"

Jack lifted his brows and admitted, "Maybe a few? I haven't been back for very long since I left for the war, at least not until we married. Father and I tended to avoid the country house since Mother died."

"If Lady Eleanor were to arrive home, what would it be like for her to go into the village? I suspect she wouldn't." It was difficult to imagine her stepmother living anywhere except London. "For me, it was never at Father's house that felt like…Christmas in the air. That was with Aunt Agatha."

"She was an extraordinary woman. For me, the holidays always required my mother to be there to feel like anything. Otherwise, Father and I just had mulled wine with our roast dinner instead of bourbon. Or perhaps both."

Violet asked, "What did your mother do to make it special?"

"One of those Christmas puddings. The flamed ones. Father and I haven't had one since Mother died."

Violet laid her head on his shoulder, the glass in the auto fogging as they chatted instead of going inside.

"Aunt Agatha made a big deal of the stockings," Violet said. "They were filled with the most magical things. Not just fruit, nuts, and sweets, but a letter from her and then little treasures. She had specially made stockings for us, so they were huge, Jack." Violet could feel her eyes shining at the memory. As a child and a girl—digging into the stocking was a glistening memory.

"What about the food?"

"You food-obsessed man," Violet laughed. "We had it all. Beef Wellington and roasted turkey. Roasted potatoes, carrots, parsnips. Aunt Agatha would order a feast fit for a king from Cook and then fill the table with guests. I always was allowed a glass of wine and sherry with Aunt Agatha after dinner. I'm craving it now, I think."

Jack kissed the back of her hand and then opened his auto door, rounding to hand her out. She adjusted the simple twill dress she'd worn. It was a dark brown with a tie at the neck that was a pretty yellow. With the brown stockings, the brown sturdy shoes, and the brown cloche, she was a bit like a slender tree trunk. There was, however, a red feather on her cloche along with quite a lovely pearl broach.

She wore a simple pearl choker about her neck, her wedding ring, and another pearl broach on her brown wool coat. She stretched while Jack took the dogs over to the green and then followed him while he threw a stick for them until they were ready to go back into the basket in the auto. As soon as the auto door closed on the dogs, Jack and Violet headed into the pub.

The fire was crackling in a hearth that could have been built two hundred years before. The hearth was made of massive stones and the mantel had been topped with garland and glass baubles. The air was scented with bread, garlic, ginger, mulled wine, and chips. A combination of traditional pub scents combined with holiday spices and flavors.

Violet glanced at the board where the day's specials were written in chalk and found that in addition to the stew Violet and Jack were looking for, there were also a few Christmas dinner items, including turkey legs, game pie, mince pie, and fruit cake.

They took a table and ordered. Violet sighed in relief to

be sitting in something that wasn't moving while Jack's head cocked and he frowned lightly.

"Mayor Potter?"

The fellow turned. His eyes were bulging a bit, and he had a ruddy nose and cheeks, and hair sprouting from his ears with mere wisps on his head. He grinned widely at Jack's face, however, and stood up, leaning on a thick cane. "Jack, my boy! How are you?"

Jack shook the man's hand and turned to Violet. "Mayor Potter, do join us. Maybe we can buy you a pint? My wife, Violet."

"Married, are you?" He winked at Violet with a merry gaze and then lifted both brows at Jack in doubt.

Jack's burst of laughter was followed by, "I'm surprised by it as well."

The age that had seemed obvious before faded away in the light of the mayor's animated chatter with Jack. He dove into telling Jack what seemed like decades of updates from people that Jack would have known, and Violet listened, watching as her husband leaned in, asked questions, and laughed at stories. The names were all foreign to Violet, but she loved the expressions that moved over his face.

She lingered over her beef stew while Jack listened and then looked up in surprise when he gasped, "Really? No!"

Violet bit her bottom lip to keep back the observation that he sounded rather like a duo of ladies gossiping about the girls they liked less. Instead, she focused more tightly when he added, "A fire? Did they live?"

Violet's gaze widened and all trace of humor left.

"They lived. No real hurts. Some coughing that'll last for a while, but hopefully not too long. Lost everything else really. What's worse—though—"

Violet hated to lean forward, so she held herself back with strict self-control.

"It's that demmed fool Cowell."

"Cowell?" Jack frowned and glanced at Violet as if she'd know. She shook her head, and he winked at her before returning to Mayor Potter.

"The new mayor. Never would have retired, would I, if I'd known the fools would vote that lad in. This is what happens when you give ladies the vote. Campaigned to him, he did. Targeted the ladies and stole my job."

"Here now," Violet said.

Mayor Potter hmphed and shot her a dark look. "He's got half the town's matrons in love with him. Our little hamlet has become a den of iniquity, betrayal, and broken vows."

"It can't be that bad, can it?" Jack asked, waving over one of the pub lads.

"Oh, can't it!" Potter snuffled and thumped his beer mug on the table for another dark ale. "It can indeed!"

Jack waited and Potter snuffled again, accepting his next mug of dark ale as his due.

"I tell you what. He started attending the ladies auxiliary meetings. Flattering them. Walking the prettiest home. Pretending as if every word that falls from their lips is brilliant."

Violet pressed her lips together to stop herself from jumping to the defense of her sex.

"Come on now, Potter," Jack argued, "that doesn't necessarily mean he's giving them other attentions."

"Perhaps not," Potter said, taking quite a large gulp of his ale, but then he said, "My Hildy isn't one to say the worst of other women, but she has nothing good to say of a few of those ladies in that club. The charitable works have fallen off, and since her husband started coming, poor Mrs. Cowell has disappeared."

Violet wasn't sure what to think of the fellow, but she wasn't going to assume that the ladies club were indulging the mayor. She doubted it fiercely. She had to admit, however, there was a part of her who very much wanted to see this ladies auxiliary club in action.

"What I was tell you, my boy," Potter said, cutting into Violet's rumination, "is that Cowell refused to use the donations for the Darcy family this year. Lost their house, all their things, and their neighbors are being asked to donate for some self-indulgent statue. Wouldn't have gone like that in my day, I tell you. Wouldn't have had to have a few of the elders of the church rebel—half because they're tired of hearing the mayor's praises sung by the ladies—and organize things instead. Now there's two sets of folks asking for money, and Cowell leans on the table a bit, doesn't he? Pressures a fellow. Makes 'em feel like they're stingy. The folks who'd have helped the poor Darcys are without funds when the elders turn up asking for a charitable giving that anyone would want to donate to."

The rage was enough to have a bit of spittle flying from the man's mouth, and he wiped his mouth with his napkin, shook his head angrily and then muttered darkly.

"That doesn't feel right, does it?" Jack asked.

"Be prepared, my boy," Potter added meaningfully, glancing at Violet and then lifting his brows dramatically.

"I can assure you," Jack told Potter easily, "some small-town mayor isn't up to persuading Violet to anything she doesn't want to do, and for some odd reason—she does love my poor self."

"Upon occasion," Violet told him starchily, "though when I don't like you, I tend to not like anyone at all."

Jack laughed, adjusting his collar, and told Potter, "I've been in a bit of trouble lately, sir. The truth is, I might need to take you aside and ask for sage advice on how to get beyond those days."

Potter laughed, glanced at Violet, and then suggested, "You're rich, aren't you? Jewelry? I hear that solves everything."

"Violet is rather spoilt in that category."

"I told you I am accepting rubies." Violet sipped her ginger ale, which she loved almost as much as ginger wine. "However, I prefer jewelry to remind me of good times rather than bad."

"Better go with something she can't just buy herself then." Potter glanced at Violet. "Afraid you're gonna have to go with the pretty words, lit candles, flower petals spread on the bed, that kind of nonsense."

Violet lifted her brows in challenge at Jack and said, "Rubies? Rose petals? Candles? I'll take it all."

"Oh ho—" Potter laughed. "Well now, careful lad. She's told you what she wants and it's when we try to side-step that fellows like that fiend Cowell slide in."

Violet shook her head and stood. Jack started to get up, and Violet shook her head. "No, no. Have fun, darling. I'm going to visit the ladies, take the dogs for a stretch, and visit that bakery across the way. Cook isn't expecting us until tomorrow, but I feel certain that some cinnamon buns and cakes will see us through until she's cooking again."

Jack snorted and Violet winked at them both, shaking Potter's hand one more time, and escaping into the street.

CHAPTER 3

*V*iolet glanced at Jack as he maneuvered down the wet road towards their country house. Despite the time at the pub, she had yet to explain what was on her mind. Jack knew she was pondering something, but given the manuscript on her lap, he most likely thought it had to do with that rather than Ginny and Geoffrey.

Violet rubbed her hand over Rouge's belly, who was lying between Vi and Jack. Holmes had taken up position on Jack's lap, and the puppies were in the basket in the back. They were nearly old enough to go to their homes, and Violet would be happy to see them gone. She really needed to watch Rouge carefully before another lot of pups ended in their laps.

Violet bit her bottom lip. "I'm concerned—"

"What about?" Jack asked, glancing at Violet and then back at the road.

"Ginny and Geoffrey." She said it with careful weight, and Jack understood immediately. The two were supposedly in love. Students in love. Not as supervised as they would be at home. They went to school near each other. Ginny's school was lax in attendance standards, allowing the students to take control of their education. Geoffrey was floundering in his relationships given that he'd learned that the earl was not, in fact, his birth father.

"Had a little conversation with Geoffrey already," Jack told Violet easily. "You're late to the party, darling Vi. Geoffrey has been told clearly and precisely with dark threats what will happen if he dabbles with our Ginny."

"Didn't Father have that same conversation with Tomas?" Violet asked him, with a lifted brow. Isolde had eloped and fled the country when she'd turned up expecting a child while still unmarried.

"Tomas was a former soldier, and they were quite a bit older. Geoffrey understands how difficult that situation would be. I think we're all right, Vi my love."

"Are we?" Violet fought a rush of relief while she examined the idea. The thought that she needed to talk to Ginny regardless of Jack's conversation struck Vi hard and fast and the relief was gone. She closed her eyes and sighed. "I think I might still need to talk to Ginny."

"You should," Jack agreed easily. "Is this on your mind because Lottie asked you for advice?"

"Am I late to that party as well?"

"Darling Vi, you're slow and out of touch. Old-fashioned as you are."

Her gaze narrowed on his smirk. Slowly she reached out to flick his ear, but before she succeeded he caught her hand and tangled their fingers. His hold was just a bit tighter than usual to prevent her from escaping and flicking him.

"How did you know?" Violet asked him. "About Lottie?"

"Gerald asked me if we were struggling or preventing a family. When I answered, he asked whether you'd help them prevent too. He's worried about springing too much on Lottie all at once, you know. Being a future countess isn't so easy, he thinks."

"It shouldn't be that hard to get this information," Violet muttered, staring out the window. "Really, though. We can't be the only couple who isn't quite ready to dive into a family. My goodness man, you were just shot! There will be no more bullet wounds before we start adding little Wakefields. If you leave me, laddie, I will desecrate your grave and find happiness in being the most spoiling aunt England has ever seen. Being a widowed mum, no thank you. It's too sad."

Jack winced and then turned the attention from him. "Let alone that sort of sick, exhausted look Victor carried for far too long. Given how easy his life is, you have to wonder what the fellows who work in mines do. Babes at home, crying all night, working all day with the heavy labor bit. That's a bleak fate."

"You're the dim one now, lad. The ladies do all the baby bits. The men probably just grouse about the noise." With a deep voice she said, "Shut that brat up, woman."

"The gents are working." Jack's tone was innocent.

"What I'm saying," Violet shot back, "is that the luxury of Victor's life and the good nature of his heart is why he could and did help. I'm sure some of those working fathers would help too, but you have to have your wits in a mine or factory."

"True enough," Jack said, kissing the back of her hand. "I'll help you when our time comes, darling, and we'll steal one of those excellent nannies."

Violet put down her manuscript, lifted Rouge onto her

lap, and scooted closer to Jack. "Parenting Ginny is hard. I don't know if I can do it again."

"Ginny is a different creature than our children will be," Jack told Violet. "Half-living on the streets, caring for her grandmother, losing her parents, being generally unsupervised. She has been through so much and matured long before you and Victor and then Kate and I were dipping our oars into life. We're far more likely to have a spoilt brat like Isolde or Geoffrey."

Violet gasped and pulled away. "Bloody hell, you're right. What a day for terrible realizations."

"We'll have to make them work, like servants," Jack suggested. "To keep them humble."

"Or do service," Violet countered. "We could take them up to the orphanage."

"No," Jack said, shaking his head. "That's putting our spoilt brats in the faces of those struggling children and making them suffer by comparison."

"Oh goodness," Violet sighed, "I hadn't thought of that. I am terrible."

"You'd have thought of it," Jack said. "You're as protective of those poor mites as anyone. Besides, Kate's mother would have stopped you."

"True," Violet agreed. She and Victor might finance much of that orphanage, but Mrs. Lancaster was the queen there.

VIOLET TOOK a long bath when they reached the country house. It was mid-afternoon and Victor and Kate had arrived, Kate declaring that her first order of business was a long soak herself, followed by quite a long nap. She had disappeared up the stairs after kissing each of Violet's cheeks. The nanny had been on holiday just before they'd arrived, and Kate had dark circles under her eyes from the babies.

Violet had taken a shorter bath in favor of a longer nap, and then she dressed in a dark green dress, with lace across the torso embellished with the shape of holly leaves within the silk.

She put on a feathered headpiece with a jaunty peacock decoration over her ear. She wrapped her black pearls around her neck, letting the loop fall to her waist, and followed it with her diamond choker and then emerald earbobs to match her dress. She carefully put rouge on her cheeks, kohl on her eyes, and mascara on her lashes. With a brilliant red lipstick on her lips, she made a kissing face, winked at herself, and tied red bows around both Rouge and Holmes's necks to add to the seasonal flair.

Dinner was a beef roast with roasted vegetables, York-shire pudding, and potted shrimps. It wasn't quite on the level of what their holiday dinner would be, but it felt festive being served with mulled wine and a cranberry trifle, and made even more so with her friends and family seated around the table.

Violet had little expectation before they'd pulled out the decorations after dinner that Lila would help. On the best of days, Lila was dramatically lazy. With a baby on the way? After a heavy dinner? The only finger she'd be lifting was the one to sip her tea.

Lila's baby belly was bulging, and she'd had an armchair carried from the parlor to the hall to watch. The baby was due in March or April, they weren't entirely certain since neither of them had realized she was with child immediately.

They just laughed and shrugged and then threw out wild guesses of when their angel would arrive. Even if their doctor had given them a timeline, Denny at least, preferred to change the answer with each subsequent time.

Vi gestured to Denny with a handful of decorations in silent command. "I prefer to watch." Denny leaned against the wall in the front hall, eggnog in hand, and glanced at Lila, who simply lifted a brow at him.

"Get some garland," Violet told Denny without equivocation, "and wrap it prettily around the banister or you'll find that the gin has dried up only for you. Add some pretty baubles or tinsel, and be artistic."

"That's no way to Christmas," he declared with woebegone eyes. "Working! Who'd have thought it would come to this? Isn't this why my dear aunt left me funds? To laze about and watch others work? No offense, Hargreaves, but I feel certain you have the touch and the eye for such things."

"None taken, Mr. Denny," Hargreaves said idly.

"No!" Violet snapped. "Aren't we having a holiday? With the trimmings? Ready yourself, laddie. You'll be hanging baubles, lighting candles, and making merry. Happy Christmas and all that," Violet said sourly and then scowled. "I did not want to say that sarcastically. Laddie, you had better watch yourself. I've got my mean eyes on."

Jack had just tied the mistletoe over the doorway to the parlor and he had no sympathy for the whining Denny. "I'm the injured one, yet you see me here, slaving away." Jack tugged Violet into the shadow of the mistletoe and kissed her soundly. She sighed into his chest and said, "You're a good lad. Unlike these two."

Victor and Denny glanced at each other, somehow transforming from married men into the schoolboys they had once been.

"My hands are full," Victor declared, juggling the babies in each arm. While Agatha looked on like the sweetling she was, Vivi grabbed Victor's ear and wrenched it. Kate had disappeared after dinner stating that she was going to bed early, despite her nap, and Victor had stared after her with concern. He glanced at Violet, and she saw something in his gaze that worried her.

All was well with Kate, wasn't it? But if it were truly wrong, he would have said something.

Violet crossed to take her namesake, Vivi. "Get to work, laddie, and give Agatha to lazy Lila."

"I'm a sacred vessel," Lila declared. "Growing an angel. These things are not done easily, you know."

Given Lila was glowing with beauty and health, Violet simply shot her a dark look. Kate had made being with child seem like a journey through the shadow of death long before the final hour. Lila, however, made it seem a bit like a dance of mayday.

Someone rang the doorbell stridently and then rang it again.

"Your child will be a demon," Victor told Lila as he crossed to the front door. Victor swung the door open and blinked in surprise as a telegram boy gestured with an envelope.

"Telegram for Mrs. Wakefield, Mr. Carlyle, or"—he blushed brilliantly—"any damn person capable of answering." The boy shuffled and avoided their gazes as he added, "That was a quote."

"Gerald does have a turn of phrase, doesn't he?" Denny asked, leaning against Lila's armchair.

"They want to know if you want to answer," the boy said.

Victor waved him in as Violet crossed to her twin, re-handing baby Vivi over and taking the envelope. She opened it and stared.

THE BRATS AREN'T HERE. TRACKING THEM
DOWN. VI, YOU'RE A DEVIL.
G. CARLYLE

CHAPTER 4

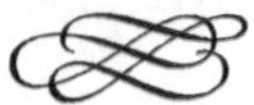

iolet read it again and then read it out loud, hearing the shock in her voice. Her hands were shaking, and she realized her mind was stumbling. It hadn't said that the children weren't where they should be. How could they be gone? How could they be missing? And just why was Violet the one who had caused this?

Well—perhaps she'd engineered him being there. Otherwise the children would have come home alone. Victor's shout of laughter had Violet shooting him a dark look.

"Do you think they aren't off on some grand adventure? They're fine."

She rubbed her chest and slowly realized he was probably right. "Those demons!"

"You are Ginny's guardian," Victor laughed again. "You'd have taken off on an adventure too. She was probably thinking, 'What would Violet do?' Then our Ginny jumped into the deep end of the pool, didn't she?"

"Not when Aunt Agatha was expecting me! I wouldn't've."

Violet winced at the lie and then muttered, "Not with a wart like Geoffrey."

Victor lifted a brow and asked, "Was I better, though? I am sure I was a wart as well."

Violet rubbed her chest where her heart was racing and breathed slowly as Victor admitted, "We'd have at least told Agatha. Even if it was too late for her to stop us."

"Jack!" Violet cursed as her panic escalated. "What do we do?"

"Sounds like a problem for Gerald. Maybe we buy him a nice bottle of bourbon?"

"You might need to give him more than that. He's going to need to recover from chasing the demons down," Denny added with a gleeful chuckle.

Violet crossed to the stairs and slumped onto a step. "I can't believe they did this."

"Can't you?" Denny asked, staring at Violet in surprise, then sank onto the step beside her. "You're the most independent woman I know. You make Lila look clingy and she rules our roost with me a mere servant and middle of the night foot warmer. Certainly, Ginny asked herself, 'What would Violet do?' To be honest, I ask myself that question rather often."

Violet breathed in slowly and blew it out, shoving Denny lightly and drawing out a high-pitched giggle. "Are you zozzled at a time like this?"

"How was I to know?" he asked defensively.

Violet turned to Jack, who pulled her to her feet and held her against his chest. "Children travel home by themselves all the time."

"They do." He rubbed his hand up and down her back, and like a baby, she was soothed.

"Which probably means there's a message on the way. Likely saying that they left early or something. Look for us at dawn, we took the night train," Violet guessed, trying to soothe herself.

Just because Ginny wasn't where they expected didn't mean that she was in trouble. She should have known that Gerald was coming for them, but perhaps she hadn't gotten the letter. That was possible. The mail tended to be rather reliable, but perhaps this one time it hadn't been?

Violet bit down on her bottom lip, fighting the worry. "We did leave London a day early. Why don't we call to the London house? Beatrice is there. Perhaps there's a letter?"

Hargreaves, who had been standing nearby with the box of pine boughs, immediately set it down and disappeared into the library. Jack's father, James, tended to spend his day among the books, next to the fire, smoking his pipe and reading, and had disappeared to the library after dinner. No doubt for quiet after the raucous meal.

She felt as though panic was clawing at her, held back by the slender thread of hope that Ginny had just missed the letter they'd sent about Gerald and Lottie bringing the two young people home. It was supposed to be fun, going back with the engaged couple, the puppies, the special basket Vi had Hargreaves put together for the journey to make the it full of the Christmas season.

Violet took a seat on the stairs again and folded herself over her legs, pressing her face into her lap, and trying to breathe through the worry. There was an idea in Vi's head that came up with every problem with Ginny, that her parents and grandmother were looking down on Violet and judging her. Vi knew the joy that Ginny added to their lives. It was overwhelming. People would tell Violet or Victor that they were so kind to have taken Ginny on. The truth was quite the opposite and Violet felt that she owed something to their parents and fate for putting such joy into her life.

"You got a message, lady?" the delivery boy asked.

Violet just held back a growl and a curse. She turned her face so she could see the room and shot Jack a dark look.

"We're going to need a few minutes," Jack told the boy. "We need to see what we know, so we can reply properly."

"I'm supposed to hurry back. Folks pay for quick delivery, and I'm the only boy on right now."

"They'll tip you well, kid." Denny glanced about and then crossed to the teacart that housed the iced eggnog. "Want some eggnog? Warm your insides against the chill and all that."

"Should we be giving him drinks?" Lila asked from her armchair. "There's so much rum in that it makes my nose burn. Though I suppose he isn't ours."

"You'll be champion parents," Victor announced, but he didn't object when Denny poured the boy an eggnog and handed it over. Violet shook her head against her knees. Her mind was buzzing, but she was aware enough to know that the child must be around fourteen years old. At the moment, Lila was right, the child wasn't theirs to worry over. Their children seemed to be missing.

Hargreaves returned a few minutes later when the tense silence had become so thick it was suffocating. "I have Beatrice on the line, ma'am."

Violet shot Victor a look that said he would be helping with the parenting side of things. They had, after all, taken Ginny on together. But he only shrugged and then rocked Vivi as Violet crossed to the library to speak with Beatrice,

Jack following. Her father-in-law gave her a concerned look as Violet picked up the telephone.

"There's a message here, Violet," Beatrice said, still stumbling over Violet's first name. Beatrice's tone echoed over the distance. "It came with the morning mail."

"Read it to me," Violet asked and followed up with a tardy, "Please."

"'Dearest Violet,'" she read, "'please don't hate me. Geoffrey needs to meet his first father and doesn't want to go alone. The story Lady Eleanor told doesn't match the story that you told us. We've gone to discover the truth and speak with him directly and see those who would have been his family. I'll be home soon. Don't worry—' there's an exclamation point after that," Beatrice added dryly. "'We'll be fine and have saved for just this. Love Ginny.'"

Violet cursed into the phone and then cursed gain. If Geoffrey had been so desperate to meet his father, why hadn't he simply told someone? Victor would have taken Geoffrey in a moment. Violet sighed deeply and then cursed once again, belatedly recalling that Jack's father was in the room.

"Did you want me to try to go after them?" Beatrice asked.

Violet wanted to say no. Christmas was mere days away, but yes, of course she did. "Try to find them, if you can. I'll make it up to you."

"Violet," Beatrice said gently. "You've taken me from housemaid to personal maid to secretary to businesswoman. There is nothing I wouldn't do for you."

Violet laughed, but she wasn't all that amused. "Darling Beatrice, you did that for yourself by being amazing. I'll make it up to you."

"I'll be on the next train," Beatrice promised. "I'll do what I can to find them. I promise."

"Gerald is looking for them too," Violet said. "Keep in touch, so we can tell you where to go. Take whatever funds you might need from the safe and multiply it by three just in case."

"I won't need that much," Beatrice protested.

Violet shook her head. Not that Beatrice could see her. Violet cleared her throat. "We have no idea where they're going, but they're high strung school children. If anyone can find trouble on an ill-advised journey across England, it's schoolboys and girls."

"They'll be all right, Vi," Jack said. "It's not like they're seven years old."

Violet's daggered glance had him lifting his hands in surrender.

"Use my name," Violet told Beatrice, "and my father's name. Hopefully it'll be a case of taking them by the ears and scolding them soundly for scaring me." Violet ended the call and then shook her head. She turned to Jack. "Beatrice is going. Ginny sent a note."

Jack opened his arms and Violet stepped into them. "They're fine." It was more to herself than to him. He didn't seem all that worried. In fact, everyone seemed to be indulging Violet. She told Jack while James listened quietly.

"They have money, Violet," Jack said gently. "The trains aren't the…the wild west of America. The men who are working those trains know that school children are traveling unattended. They keep an eye out. Ginny and Geoffrey might end where we don't want them to be, but they won't get in any real trouble. Geoffrey's—" He trailed off because Violet objected to the term 'real' father. The earl had been the one who raised Geoffrey and looked after him. Not that fellow. "Fitzhugh wasn't so bad. He'll send them home and all will be fine and when we box their ears, they'll think better of their choices next time."

Violet sighed and nodded. Knowing they weren't kidnapped but off on a stupid adventure did relieve that rush of panic. James gave her an encouraging look that suggested he'd been through the same with his children more than once, and she took heart in that. Jack had turned out all right, after all.

When she reached the hall again, she found Denny carefully putting up the garland, and Victor was waiting with a large wineglass full of mulled ginger wine.

Geoffrey was a bit of an idiot and a wart, and this act had infuriated Violet, but Ginny was as clever as they came. Without question Ginny would be all right and she'd get Geoffrey out of whatever trouble he led them into.

"Fools," Violet muttered. She looked at the delivery boy, who had ceased to object over waiting with the eggnog, and said, "Send back that they've gone to the," she sighed and ground out, "real father's homestead for a face-to-face."

The boy paused and Jack wrote it out for him, paid him, and probably over-tipped him even after waiting, but Vi supposed it was Christmas.

"I'm going to hold this over Ginny's head for years to come," Violet swore before turning to Victor. She took Vivi back, lifting an imperious brow. "You were of no help."

"I held the baby and got you wine."

"You can telephone Lady Eleanor and explain. Leave Ginny out of it."

Victor paled, but Violet left him and the decorating to lie down on the Chesterfield in the parlor. She had one of the babies, her special wine that Victor had made for her, and she needed to breathe until she felt the panic fully pass.

Vivi pushed up and examined Violet with big eyes that matched Vi's own. Vivi cooed and then blinked slowly before she laid her head down on Violet's chest.

Violet rocked the baby instinctively as she breathed in and out. It was all right. The children weren't kidnapped. They were just dumb. They had money. They were going to a safe little village. It was the opposite way of the country house, but they weren't diving into the docks near London or shanghaied or something equally horrible.

"You sure you want to miss this?" Denny asked from the doorway. "Hargreaves is connecting Victor now to Lady Eleanor."

"Yes," Violet said, rubbing Vivi's back. "I won't sympathetically carry some of her tongue lashing. This way only Victor suffers, and I avoid."

"I like you how you think, darling Vi," Denny announced. "May I be done with the garland now?"

"No," Violet said without opening her eyes, but she could picture the woeful expression she was sure he sent her way.

CHAPTER 5

"Violet darling," Jack's father, James, said the next morning. "The mayor and the ladies from the auxiliary club are here."

"All right," Violet said, glancing up from her manuscript and then immediately sinking back into it.

"They expect you to serve them tea and chat with them until they ask for a donation. I have to admit, it is a burden I am happy to hand over."

"Can't we just give it to them now?" Violet asked, still in her story more than she was in the present. She'd had a moment of curiosity at the idea of the mayor, but the crime in her own novel was bright in Violet's mind, and it was a difficult state to reach.

James shook his head. "The mayor and his gaggle of local wives will be offended. All the important ones are here. The vicar's wife, the mayor's wife, the mayor's mother-in-law, the head of the ladies auxiliary. Who else could be here? I suppose we could count Father Christmas amongst us, since the mayor is to play him. To be honest, I don't know. I'm just glad it's you, darling, and not I."

Violet grinned at him, blinking herself into the present. "A gaggle?"

He grinned unrepentantly. "A gaggle. Also Ham and Rita have arrived, just moments before. Rita's father is here as well."

"Oh!" Violet stood then, and when he grinned at the change in her attitude she admitted, "I have missed Rita. That Ham timed his arrival at the same time is just interesting, isn't it?"

"Interesting? He's a clever detective, our Ham."

"How many trains do you think he let go through before he found her?"

"Every train of the day," her father-in-law shot back. "Should be an interesting holiday. Rita brought her father—"

"Oh, did she!" Violet rubbed her hands together. "It'll be fun to see how he interacts with Ham while we're all watching."

"They're changing and getting comfortable from their travels. So you have time—"

"Don't leave me with the locals! I understand the mayor is a ladies' man."

He grinned and then took a sideways sidle. "You can handle it, darling Vi."

Oh! He was going to leave her with them. He might have handed over the country house to Violet and Jack, but it was James who everyone knew, not Vi.

"I'll send you Jack, shall I?"

"Send me whoever you can," Violet muttered, knowing from James's gleeful expression, he was not going to join her in the parlor. If Ginny left Violet feeling as though she were playacting at being in charge, moments like the one before her left her feel as though she were suffocating at being the lady of the house. It was the equivalent of a Dickens scenario that would end with Scrooge throwing out the supplicants.

Violet lingered just long enough to give her father-in-law time to get her any kind of support and then she made her way to the parlor. The tea arrived just as Violet did, and she pasted a welcoming smile on her face. She had no objections to charitable giving or even the neighbors—just the awkward interaction where they found their footing.

Her guests had seated themselves while they were waiting for Violet to arrive, and she gestured to them to keep their seats.

"Hello," she said brightly, smiling around the room.

She paused as she realized that the room was full of women, at least eight of them, and so the single man stood out. He wore a fine suit and had taken the seat near the fire that Jack or his father would normally enjoy. Around him like flower petals were the ladies. Each wore fine dresses, cosmetics perfectly applied.

Before Violet could introduce herself, Jack stepped into the room followed by Denny and Lila. Despite Jack's entrance, the mayor took control. "Mayor Cowell," he introduced himself with a hearty laugh. He gave first one lady then another a warm look as though it were meant just for her, introducing each with various sweet smiles for the lady, and Violet caught the not-so-well-hidden looks of jealousy that the women cast one another. She felt as though she needed to head back to the pub, apologize to the former mayor, and buy him another round of dark ale.

"Mr. Cowell!" Jack said heartily with a forced smile, interrupting the introductions and taking control at the same time. With Jack's penetrating gaze, Violet had little doubt that her love had seen the same things that Violet noticed.

"This is my wife, Violet," Jack said. "And our good friends Denny and Lila Lancaster who are spending the holidays with us."

The mayor nodded politely and took over the conversation again to finish with his personal tour of each lady present with a look and a name, bypassing only his mother-in-law, who got a sour look.

Was the man aware that he gave away his feelings with his expressions and tone? With every woman listed, except his mother-in-law, the named woman smiled charmingly first to Mr. Cowell and only after to Violet, Jack, and their friends. Violet almost felt as though she'd stepped between a betrothed couple mere days before their wedding. None of the people were, however, married to each other.

Violet ignored the mayor, who had started his prepared speech with wide, dimpled grins and laughs at his own jokes, and turned to the mother-in-law.

"What was your name again?"

The mayor quite deliberately interrupted, "My mother-in-law."

"Joan Oates," the older woman said with a glint of appreciation for Violet, who refused to be part of the mayor's slighting. Her knitting needles clinked her in hand as Violet nodded at her, taking in the sight of what looked to be quite a lovely white baby blanket.

"Oh, didn't I say?" Mr. Cowell asked, knowing he hadn't. He smiled charmingly at Violet, flashing those dimples like weapons. If only he knew that his lingering gaze made Violet sick to her stomach.

"You're playing Father Christmas?" Violet asked, and the

gaggle of ladies tittered. Sarcastically, Violet said, "Surely that can't be right."

Joan Oates snorted and Denny giggled. Violet winked when everyone else turned their attention to the mayor.

"Coming on a bit strong," Denny whispered, not bothering to truly lower his tone, so Violet, Joan, and two of the women just beyond heard. "A bit catty for the season, my love. Christmas peace and all that."

"I am a bit young," the mayor laughed heartily, missing Violet's sarcasm. His laugh was echoed by all the ladies except his mother-in-law, who snorted again. "But I'm something of the father of the town, so who better but me to look after our people?"

Joan Oates muttered again and Vi heard, "Young?" She wished she could have heard the rest. As it was, Violet had to bite down on her bottom lip to prevent her laugh, but Denny didn't bother.

"So nice of you to visit," Violet lied, and choked on a laugh when Joan Oates hissed, "Liar."

"And I wished to invite you, particularly, to our little village play," the mayor said, letting his gaze trace over Violet's body. She paused as she saw the lasciviousness in his gaze. He met her eyes and smiled slowly, as though they didn't have an audience.

Violet had to dig her fingers into her hand to keep herself from a tirade. This would be their country home, Violet told herself, and likely where they would spend most of their time when they added children to their life. She wasn't going to ring the mayor's ears with a tirade and then have to deal with him every other time she entered the village.

"I've heard tales of your cleverness," the mayor told her, ignoring Jack, Denny, and Lila. Mr. Cowell rubbed his beard carefully and she wanted to tell him to turn his eyes from her.

"Have you?" Violet asked darkly.

"A cleverness only matched by your generosity and beauty. James is a lucky man to have you as part of his family."

"I'm the lucky man," Jack said, cutting off the mayor.

It wasn't the mayor's compliments that were bothersome —though they were—it was his eyes. She felt the need to tug up her bodice and lower her hem, but it was a high-necked, collared piece with scalloped hems that, despite the rising hemlines in fashion, reached her mid-calf. She was fully covered, and it was clear that he was imagining her quite explicitly.

"Always liked your husband," Joan told Violet, cutting off her son-in-law as he tried to restart his speech. He sputtered when Mrs. Oates spoke loudly enough to silence him. "He was the clever one as a boy. I'm not surprised in the least he married a woman who matched his wit."

Violet grinned at Joan. "Exceeded, I think you mean."

"Naturally," Mrs. Oates agreed. "Ladies do have to use our wits and cleverness to get what we want, don't we?" She glanced tellingly at her son-in -law and said to Violet, loudly, "Your Jack always struck me as a bit territorial."

It was a warning to her son-in-law that had his cheeks burning. He flashed Violet those oversized dimples and a bright eye.

A lady next to him made a comment about the weather, but she was over-shadowed by another woman who leaned towards Violet and said earnestly, "It isn't just your Mr. Wakefield that is so clever, Mrs. Wakefield. Our dear Mr. Cowell is just brilliant in our play. He wrote it himself, you know. Wrote it, stars in it, directed it, gathered the donations to put it on. Our hamlet is blessed to have him for our own."

Violet smiled woodenly while Denny and Joan muttered in unison. Jack snorted at whatever Denny said, and Violet asked, "Tea anyone?" before the mayor had an apoplectic fit. He seemed surprised that Violet and Jack weren't impressed, and Vi had little doubt they'd be described as snobbish. Perhaps they might be snobbish, Violet thought, but they didn't care about class so much as wit, and the mayor was far prouder of his than he should be.

"Got any whiskey for that tea?" Joan murmured and was overheard by everyone in the room. Several of the gaggle gasped and her son-in-law tried to laugh the comment off, but Violet glanced at Denny, who grinned and crossed to the bar, bringing back the decanter.

"Bourbon would be better, I think," Violet told her. "With the blend of black tea, lapsang souchong, orange zest, and vanilla. It's quite lovely with a splash of bourbon and honey."

"Oh, I don't think we need that," Mr. Cowell said, but his tone was an order to Violet that had her biting back a rude reply. He seemed to have forgotten that this was her house.

CHAPTER 6

"Unwise," Denny said, shaking his head. "Better to obey Violet whenever she gets that look on her face," Denny whispered to Joan as he handed Violet the bourbon. "Violet might be the daughter of an earl, but she's a guttersnipe in her soul. Our Vi holds a mean grudge."

Joan Oates laughed and then nodded her head towards the woman just next to the mayor. "Bernadette Lovell. Married not even a year. Wouldn't want to be her when her husband realizes she's stepping out on him. Bit of a hot head he is, and well in love with her. He'll be furious."

Violet pressed her lips together as she made Joan a cup of tea just as Violet described, heavy on the bourbon, light on the tea.

"The one next to her," Joan said, "wants tea and lemon. No milk, no honey. She's been sour herself since the mayor started preferring young Mrs. Lovell."

The mayor heard the whispering and the woman just next to Joan Oates was casting scandalized looks their direction. Vi made the tea as Joan suggested and handed it to Denny to deliver. She made the mayor a tea and then went around the room pouring and flavoring teas as requested, ignoring the mayor every time he tried to take up the reins of the conversation.

The mayor crossed to her to accept his plain tea with a commiserating smile as though apologizing for trying to control Violet. "We try to be particularly circumspect during the holidays. Set a good example to our lesser neighbors who need a bit of a helping hand and a guiding light."

"Until someone is watching," Joan muttered low. "Then he drowns himself in cheap whiskey."

"How circumspect you are with your plain tea then," Violet told him, ignoring his failed attempt to make things up. "I fear the holiday punch, eggnog, and mulled wine flows rather heavily in our home during the holiday season."

"Well you don't have children, do you?" the woman just next to Joan asked sourly. "These bright young things who flit about setting poor examples don't have to worry about the upcoming generation." The woman smiled smoothly and Violet had to wonder if she was the vicar's wife or an old maid. Either way, the woman's tight-lipped smile and judgement-filled eyes made Violet want to fill her cup with nothing but whiskey.

Instead, Violet said, "We expect three children here. I find that drinks flowing freely doesn't mean that we need to get so zozzled we can't tell the difference between good behavior and bad. In fact," Violet told the woman flatly, glancing at the mayor for good measure, "I find that bad behavior comes from our choices rather than our drinks. If, after all, one knows that they're mean while imbibing, they could simply choose to enjoy our very good ginger beer, pineapple juice, and fizzy drinks."

"Too true," Mr. Cowell said smarmily, "and it's always good to look after our elders especially in their dottier years." His cruel look to his mother-in-law had Joan draining her cup.

Joan held out her teacup and Violet didn't bother with the tea for the refill. Violet lifted a brow at the mayor until he moved away from her.

Mrs. Oates took her teacup of bourbon and whispered to Violet, "You are delightful."

The mayor returned to the circle of ladies smiling prettily at him while Denny and Mrs. Oates competed for naughtiness. Lila, on the other hand, yawned, and Jack watched it all, probably taking in more than Violet by far.

"We've a few projects in hand, you know," the mayor announced once again, spreading a wide, engaging grin that Violet had little doubt he practiced in the mirror. "For our little hamlet. Gathering money for those who struggle as well as a few things that our local hall needs. No need to lose our respect of self and let things go to ruin."

"I've always thought the town hall looks lovely," Violet told him. "Along with the green and the town square."

"They're all lovely," Joan said, draining her cup when her son-in-law shot her a quelling look. "New everything. This village needs more money like I need to be looked after. Unlike other families."

"It's important to stay on top of these things," the mayor laughed again, sending his mother-in-law a dark look that even Violet saw promised revenge.

Violet shot Jack a look that commanded a donation and a foisting. She was bored and wanted to murder the mayor a time or two in her book. Perhaps she'd fictionalize Joan and turn her into a heroine who saved her daughter from the villain-mayor.

"You'd do better to donate to your own charities rather than this one," Joan muttered to Violet. "I wouldn't give that man two-pence."

"Are you always so helpful?" Violet whispered back as Mr. Cowell went on about adding some art to the foyer of the town hall and a statue to the green.

"I only came to watch him try to add you to his string," Joan whispered to Violet, any attempt at holding her tongue ruined by the whiskey. "Couldn't imagine the daughter of an earl falling for some second-rate village's cock of the walk, but I knew what he was thinking the minute he put on the slimming pin-striped suit. Fool. He lingers over that beard with tiny scissors inches from the mirror."

Violet choked on her reaction, but she wasn't surprised. She'd seen the lust in the man's gaze. Everyone had. She was only surprised he seemed to think he had a chance. Did he really think she'd cuckold Jack with a man twice her age? At Christmas? Under Jack's penetrating gaze? Jack missed nothing in general. When it came to Violet, he was almost preternatural in his ability to understand and predict her.

The mayor turned his attention to adding a statue to the town square and Violet demanded, "Do you have any projects that are less improvement and more charitable? Jack and I prefer our donations, at this time of year especially, to be for things like injured soldiers, widows, children, and the hungry."

"Ah—" His face flushed, and he guessed—rightly—that they'd been warned about his desire to slide in before the others could try to help that family with the burnt home.

"There was a family," Joan Oates cut in, shooting her son-in-law a nasty look, "whose home has burnt. A few of the town elders are spear-heading donations to help them do the repairs and get clothes and such. Mr. Banks and Mr. Harris are working to help them get their home repaired."

The mayor shifted. "They're doing their own collecting; as for the statute—"

Jack cleared his throat. "We'll add a few pounds to your statue collection, Cowell. As Violet said, the bulk of our holiday giving is best slated for the family who has lost so much rather than some less necessary piece of art. I fear we must bring this delightful chat to an end. We have an appointment." The last was an unadulterated lie and Violet stood, helping the elderly Joan Oates to her feet.

"I hope I might call on you, Mrs. Oates," Violet told her. The woman's gaze widened and she shook her head a little helplessly. "Or invite you for tea sometime. I feel certain you'd enjoy my brother."

"Yes, of course," Mrs. Oates said, relaxing at the alternative. "That does sound lovely. My daughter wasn't able to come today, but I think you'd like her as well."

Violet kissed Mrs. Oates's cheek and said low, "If she's anything like you, I feel certain I will."

Mr. Cowell cleared his throat, and Violet and Joan glanced towards him. He held out his hand and Violet reluctantly held out her own. He took her hand between both of his, letting his fingers--hidden by his other massive paw--caress her wrist. "Such a pleasure."

Violet yanked her hand free and said, "It was certainly interesting. Good day."

Vi stepped back, forcing his mother-in-law with her and

then offered, "Shall I have my man run you home, so you don't have to carry on with the same visits?"

"I had intended to walk," Joan admitted, shooting the mayor a scathing look. "Thankfully, I don't live with my poor daughter and granddaughters."

"Then I'll have my man drive you home. It's a bit chilly for a long walk, isn't it? And we're rather remote here."

"I'm stronger than I look," Joan told Violet, ignoring the dark look from her son-in-law and the titters of his gaggle. "Especially of stomach."

"The way you proceed with such a pain in the head," Violet said wickedly. "It's admirable."

"The stomach. The head. The neck. The back. The behind," Joan agreed and her laugh was dark. "This is what comes from raising daughters to make their own minds and forgetting to apply logic lessons or even a little forethought. Sucked in by a pretty smile and the idea that anyone would behave with a dash of morals."

She told her son-in-law she was accepting the offer of a ride to return home and left before the others. Violet slapped a smile on her face and tucked herself next to Jack as the women left. Each of them gave Violet an arch look or a sour glance before sliding out. Violet heard one comforting the mayor as they left with the words, "Snobbish, really. Off with you, love, these privileged types don't give, you know. They pretend and then stand on their laurels, telling themselves that the needy are lazy."

Violet would have snapped, but Hargreaves cleared his throat imperiously and gestured to the door as if he were shooing a fouled dog out the door. Vi met Jack's gaze and he shook his head, muttering, "We've really got to give that man a raise."

CHAPTER 7

*V*i stared after the locals and then told Jack, "I feel like I stepped into a…a…Trollop novel where there are generations of backstory. What was that?"

"That, my darling Violet, was coveting your neighbor's wife." Denny's dry voice was paused by escaping into the breakfast room where they'd set up far too many beverages. She could hear him a moment later hacking at the ice, and he reappeared with icy cups of eggnog for them all.

"Joan said something about Father Christmas adding me to his string. Did he really think he could? I mean—he's my father's age, at the least."

"He had a slew of other men's wives with him, Violet," Jack said, sounding disgusted. "I saw you chasing fairies when their names were listed, but his own wife wasn't among them."

"She's probably sick of him," Violet muttered. "I like his mother-in-law, however. Joan's my favorite. If it had been Joan asking for money, I'd have pulled out my checkbook and written a check for whatever she was pursuing. And if her daughter is like her, Father Christmas is probably lucky he's not being poisoned slowly."

Jack's brows lifted and Denny rubbed his hands together at the idea. "Now you know not to step out on Violet, Jack. Or if you do and you start feeling low, flee to the country without her and bring a doctor with you."

"Father Christmas had plans for you, Violet," Lila said lazily. "I feel quite besmirched just by watching. I believe I shall have to take a bath this afternoon."

Violet rolled her eyes and turned away from them both. Hargreaves stepped into the hall and cleared his throat.

"Two telegrams arrived while you were occupied, ma'am."

Violet's stomach dropped, and she held out her hand. The first was from her oldest brother:

THEY'RE A DAY AHEAD. ALREADY GONE.
TRYING TO FIND WHICH TRAIN. G.C.

Vi cursed and glanced at Jack. "Should we go after them? How can they just be gone?"

Jack took her hand and tugged her close, wrapping her up in his strong arms, as he said, "Maybe you should read the next telegram before we decide."

FOR SOME REASON THEY TOOK TRAIN TO
CLACTON-ON-SEA. FOLLOWING. WILL
TELEPHONE. B.

Violet rubbed her brow. "Clacton-on-Sea? What? Why? I —why would they go there?"

"The way she phrased it makes me wonder." Denny

shrugged when they all turned on him. "I'm only saying, she didn't say they bought tickets. Gerald can't find where they went. The ticket person would tell him if he asked. He'd just have to lean on his knuckles and emphasize his name, and he'd get whatever information he needed and two school children, a girl and a boy, traveling? Someone would have noticed."

Violet nibbled her bottom lip, unsurprised that Denny found the mischief in the small amount of information they had. She did, however, think he might have pinned it just right. With a glance at Jack, she noted he thought the same.

"So you think that Beatrice figured out that they hopped a train? They could hop off anywhere." Violet ran her hands over her face. "We should go after them."

If they left, however, who would be here if Ginny arrived home? Who would answer telegrams and telephone calls?

Violet bit down on her bottom lip. Ginny would want to come to them, wouldn't she? Ginny loved the country house. Jack's cousins were home, and Ginny had traveled with the girls to the continent. Vi knew Ginny wanted to see them.

Fiddling with her wedding ring, feeling like she was trying to dive into the untranslatable mind of a schoolgirl, Violet started to pace. She wasn't sure she'd be able to guess what Ginny would do even if Vi were also a schoolgirl.

"She's so different than I was." Violet stretched her neck and went to Jack to breathe him in, trying to let the warmth of him calm her down. "You are right. She has skills I might not have right now, but it's been a while since she's needed them."

"Gerald, Lottie, Beatrice, and—if I have my guess—Smith are after them," Jack said gently. "Someone needs to be here, manning our telephone in case they call for help and in residence in case they appear. Violet, I know you're worried, but I don't think we need to be. Are they being troublesome? Yes, but they should be all right. Clacton-on-Sea isn't a gutter."

"Do you really think Smith is there too?" Violet felt a rush of relief at the idea. It wasn't that Violet didn't trust Beatrice, but she could guess that Gerald was fed up with chasing the school children. Smith, however, was devious. Like Jack, Smith saw patterns that the upstanding would entirely miss. And he seemed to enjoy this sort of game.

"Smith?" Denny asked and then laughed. "He does keep a weather eye on our Beatrice. If he realized she was planning on chasing school children across the whole of England, he'd follow."

"He'd also be the one who realized you could travel by train without a ticket, unlike poor Gerald," Violet muttered. "Ginny has an allowance, and she doesn't spend it willy nilly. She should have money with her. Do you think they were robbed? Why wouldn't they buy a ticket?"

"I think you are borrowing trouble," Jack told her. "There's no way to know, but surely they'd send for help if they were truly without money." He glanced at Hargreaves and asked, "Gather up Victor, will you, Hargreaves?"

Violet paced again, nibbling on her thumb. She glanced up the stairs. They really had done a good job of the decorating when she'd abdicated to rub Vivi's back in the parlor. The garland was wound around the banister, and baubles and garland hung over many of the doorways. With the tinsel, the hall and grand staircase glistened.

Violet sighed as she looked at it all. She had wanted Ginny to come home to a house full of Christmas spirit. Now Violet wanted to wring the girl's neck. She told herself to breathe in slowly and exhale, but she couldn't. She left them in the hall and wandered to the parlor, still biting her thumb. She was aware that Jack eyed her with concern and Denny with humor, and Vi ignored them both.

Absently, Violet straightened the pillows in the parlor, put used teacups and saucers on the teacart, and generally tidied the room. Once it was in order, she paced back and forth behind the Chesterfield. It didn't take long for Lila and Rita to appear. They watched her pace silently, and Violet was both aware of their presence and grateful for their silence.

She finally turned to them and spoke her thoughts aloud. "She was nearly homeless and wild on the streets of London when she was far smaller."

"She was," Lila said. "I'll never forget those early sightings of her. I thought that she certainly had some sort of shiv at the ready."

Violet laughed and then her thoughts turned dark. The days of Ginny needing to carry a weapon were past. Would she have what she needed now? If they were hopping trains, why?

"Schoolgirls are stupid," she announced. "Ginny probably thinks that because she wrote me a note, I won't worry."

"She probably knows that you'll worry," Rita inserted, smiling at Vi's startled look of welcome. Vi had yet to greet Rita, but they were good enough friends that Violet was forgiven. "And she probably is more worried about Geoffrey. Schoolgirls are stupid. Foolish and likely to do things like allow themselves to get into trouble while attempting to help someone they care about."

Violet pressed her hand over her stomach. Rita didn't even know that Ginny and Geoffrey were claiming to be in love. The worry was bubbling, her mind was racing, and she felt as though she might never have children herself with the worry and helplessness Ginny engendered.

"Should we just get in the auto and motor to Clacton-on-Sea?" Vi paused to glance at her two friends.

"It would be excellent fun," Rita said. "I'm game."

"The last thing I'm doing is leaving this house before the baby arrives. That last journey about killed me. Me and my lad, we're not moving until Spring. Apologies, Violet, if you didn't intend to let us stay so long." She cast Rita an idle glance. "You are game to escape Ham because you carry a mean grudge. You should just give in. I think we're all tired of it."

"I threw my heart at his feet," Rita snapped at Lila, ignoring her joking. "What would you know about that? Denny has worshipped you since you were as young and stupid as Ginny."

"Don't say that," Violet moaned. She was not prepared for Ginny to have found her life-long love. The girl hadn't finished school; she couldn't be in a love that would last a lifetime.

Violet thought of herself at the same age, imagined a younger Jack in her life, and knew she'd have dove into so much trouble with him.

"He tossed my heart back," Rita said, unaware of Violet's internal struggles. "How can I trust him to keep it this time? He regretted throwing my love aside and assumed he could simply reel me back in at his convenience."

"You carry a mean grudge," Lila repeated. "And your pride is seething. Can we just admit it's your pride now and—"

Rita's daggered, cold glance had Lila reconsidering her words.

"Girls," Violet tried, but Lila spoke over her.

"Obviously not bypassing her pride." Lila's lazy voice finished with, "I am the idiot. Not you. Never you. What do I know about forgiving fools—married to the biggest fool of them all—and finding happiness? Nothing. Nothing at all."

Violet groaned and then shot them both a quelling look. "If we're going to be talking about idiots," Violet said, "we can start with Jack, who was shot, Ham, who nearly died—"

"Nearly died?" Rita asked in a cool low fury. Her voice could have been a blade made of ice, slicing them both.

Lila and Violet exchanged worried glances and then Lila asked, "You didn't tell her?"

"I was panicked about Jack and dealing with Eleanor." Violet avoided Rita's gaze and gave Lila a panicked look. Rita's fury had gone from hurt to seething, and Violet wouldn't have been surprised to see the woman's hair set aflame.

"You should have told her," Lila said, innocently. "She deserved to know."

"You don't know how to write?" Vi snapped at Lila. "Am I the only one who can communicate?"

"Ham almost died," Rita cut in furiously. "What do you mean?"

"There was a confrontation," Violet said. "I have not gotten the details because I don't want to imagine it up in my head. Ham was at risk, Jack helped, Ham was fine, Jack got shot. The end."

"The end?" Rita closed her eyes, and Violet noted her friend's hand shaking. "That is not the end."

Violet wasn't feeling particularly kind, so she said, "This is what love feels like, Rita. If you didn't love him, you wouldn't want to murder him right now."

Lila rubbed her stomach and told them both. "I'd feel

sorry for you, but I don't. They're both all right. They're both good men. Why are you upset, Rita? You were snubbing Ham earlier today. Do you love him or don't you?"

"He's a supervisor," Rita said hotly. "He should be in an office. Not in danger."

"Yes, well, he wasn't," Lila answered. "He was in the field and it was dangerous."

Violet glanced between her two friends. "We need chocolate, cocktails, and coffee. Shall we pause and remember we love each other?"

"I love you," Rita growled to Violet and Lila. "I even like you most of the time."

"I think you're a fool," Lila told Rita lazily. "But I appreciate that. I love you as well."

Violet groaned. "We're done. Rita, talk to Ham about what happened if you choose, but I'll remind you he's well enough to stalk you into the train station and ensure he was on your journey. He loves you. You know he does."

Rita blushed deeply, her golden hair and peaches and cream complexion setting off the flush.

"May we return to Ginny and Geoffrey? Perhaps we'll fight less." Violet faced Rita and asked, "Have you ever done anything like Geoffrey and Ginny have?"

Rita nodded, avoiding Violet's gaze. The flush hadn't faded, and her stance hadn't eased.

Vi didn't think the avoided gaze was because of the recent argument. "Were you all right? On your ill-advised adventure."

"I was—"

Violet knew the hesitation was because things could have gone bad. She didn't need Rita to provide the details. "What would you do? Based on your experience?"

"If you knew where she was, I'd say you should go get her. But you don't know. I heard Jack tell Victor that he thought you should stay here in case she appears or sends for help."

Violet fiddled with her fingers and then admitted, "I won't feel better until they're back and safe."

She crossed to the bell and rang for Hargreaves, who must have been hovering nearby because he arrived at once. She needed coffee to think. Coffee and a plea to the universe, God, or whoever was listening, that her ward would be located.

CHAPTER 8

The telephone rang a few hours later, and Violet gasped. She leapt out of her chair and darted from the parlor to the library. Hargreaves was already answering it when Violet darted in, and she cast him pleading eyes. Please, she thought, please be Ginny.

"Wakefield House," Hargreaves said, but he wasn't impervious as usual, and his normally ponderous tone was quick.

"Miss Beatrice," he said a moment after listening and then added, "I have Mrs. Wakefield here."

Violet took the receiver from him. "Beatrice! Have you found her?"

"Yes, ma'am. Well—we're getting them. They're here, and we're tracking them down. It should only take a short while according to Mr. Smith."

"Beatrice—" Violet nearly collapsed, she was so relieved, and then looked up. Victor, Jack, Kate, Rita, Ham, Denny, and Hargreaves were all staring anxiously. She had no idea when they had all appeared. "Are you sure?"

"Yes, ma'am," Beatrice replied. "I'm sure we've got them, though they've led us on quite a chase." She paused for a moment and then admitted in a low tone, "I don't know if I could have located them on my own, to be honest. They're here, though, and we'll find them. There are folks at the train station who are watching for them. They'll take them into hand, so to speak, if they're seen there. We know where they're going. The question really is if they've beat us there and left again, but Mr. Smith is checking while I telephone and watch High Street."

Tears were burning in Violet's eyes. She was in a duality of emotion and struggling to process it. It was rage, love, worry, gratitude, and sickness all at once.

"Just breathe, Vi," Jack's father said. She hadn't realized he was in the room, but he may well have been there when Hargreaves answered the telephone. James gently took the receiver from her and arranged for Beatrice to contact them as soon as they had Ginny and Geoffrey in hand.

Violet looked up at everyone else and Jack laughed a little. "It's all right," he told her. "She's all right."

"I'm going to murder her," Violet told him seriously. "Slowly."

"After you hug her?" James asked quietly, his dark eyes squinting with humor. She saw the relief in his gaze as well. "She's all right. Your brother is all right. Things will be all right, in the end, Violet dear."

"I'll just squeeze her too hard and put us out of our misery." Violet's hands were shaking in relief.

"I believe," Victor said, "that it is your turn to update Lady Eleanor."

Violet's expression was dark and unamused. Her? Violet did most of the hard things when it came to Ginny. He had well and truly better guess that this was not one of the things she was going to take on herself.

"She's mean," Victor whined, knowing Violet would leave Lady Eleanor unapprised rather than make the telephone call herself.

"Suck it up, laddie," Kate told him in Lila's general tone.

"I don't want to," Victor tried again. "Jack, you do it."

Jack only lifted a brow and Victor cursed.

"Should we go get her?" Violet asked, ignoring Victor's hedging. "They've got her pinned in that village they think."

"No," Jack told Violet. "No, Beatrice can bring them back and Smith is more than capable of wrangling Geoffrey should he protest."

"But I don't want to talk to her," Victor tried again. "I'll go get Ginny. How about that? Ham will come with me, won't you, old boy?"

"No," Ham told Victor flatly. "If Geoffrey sidesteps, Smith is the best man to take care of it."

"Is he?" Victor demanded. "Surely it should be you and I?"

"Smith will put the fear of God in Geoffrey," Ham said. "In fact, we should probably leave the spoilt wart in Smith's hands for as long as possible."

Violet ignored them all. Her hands were shaking and she was crying, and she needed to have eyes on Ginny, possibly have the girl shackled to Beatrice before Vi would truly feel all right. She hadn't realized how tightly she was being wound while not knowing where Ginny was. The rush of relief was overwhelming.

"This is what is going to happen," James declared. "Victor, you are going to contact your stepmother. Make sure she doesn't invite herself here. We will not let her through the door. When Gerald contacts us, tell him to come here to bring Geoffrey home as none of us are going to step into that role, and he clearly can't simply be put on the train and sent home.

"Violet," James continued, "you will try a hot bath, my dear. It's been a hard few days. Your Beatrice is utterly reliable and that Smith fellow can be counted on when he's on your side. There's no reason left to worry."

Violet stared at him and then thought, it couldn't hurt. She wasn't going to stop worrying until this was over, but a bath, salts, hot water, maybe a snuggle in her bed with Rouge and Holmes. Definitely necessary.

"Jack," James said to his son, "we have to go to that play tomorrow and pretend to enjoy ourselves. Give money to the fellows for the burnt house and put on a smiling face and then come back here for a Happy Christmas."

"Cowell wants money for a statue and other bits that are unnecessary," Jack grumbled. "All the while there is some family whose home burned down."

James blinked and then muttered something about that fool Cowell. "He's making enemies when he sidelines the money people give around the holidays for his pet projects. Of all the ridiculously greedy moves, to put up some statue when there's a homeless family. I would bet that many who gave assumed it would help that family. I heard from a chum of mine that he thought there was something odd in the village finances, to be honest, but I don't want to be involved."

Violet left while they were discussing finances, audits, and options. She turned when she reached her bedroom door at the sound of a quiet footfall and found that Rita had followed. Violet left the door open for her.

If the master bedroom at her London house was oversized—and it was—the one in this house was so large it was ridiculous. At some point in time, the wall between the master and mistress rooms had been removed, so two oversized rooms had been turned into one that was half the length of the house. The first time Violet had seen it, she had laughed. And then there was the bed, large enough for two families to sleep in and it hardly filled the space, so other furnishings had been added. A family could live in the master bedroom rather comfortably.

When Rita walked into the room, she turned in a slow circle. "I thought my family was ridiculous."

"Your family is ridiculous." Violet shot Rita a telling glance.

Rita shrugged.

Violet waited.

"I need help," Rita finally confessed. "I love Ham. And he knows it. And he's being patient, and I'm just—hurt and angry and I'm having a hard time not wanting to…to…sock him a good one every time I see his smug face, but I'm afraid he's going to get sick of me and my endless anger. I don't know how to let it go. Vi—" Rita bit down on her bottom lip and admitted, "I've had a hard time letting anyone into my life after my mother died. I know how hard it is to lose someone, and I shut down. You wouldn't let me and I'm glad for that, so glad that I began letting others in, too. Then I took a risk with Ham, and he hurt me so deeply. That's not gone just because he regrets turning me away. I understand he was trying to be loving, but he was wrong, and it hurt, and I'm afraid."

Violet eyes were burning for her friend, and she opened her arms wide. Rita stepped into the embrace.

"How do I stop being so angry? How do I let it go? How do I heal and love him?"

"Have you told him all of that?" Violet asked low and gentle.

Rita shook her head slowly.

Violet sank down into one of the large chairs and tugged Rita down into another. "I don't know how to tell you how to get through that much anger, but I can tell you how I try to get through my blue days."

Rita's eyes were wide.

"I journal. All my thoughts. The good and the bad. I write it all out as though I'm purging. There's magic in writing, though I can tell by your face that you don't believe me."

Rita laughed a watery sound.

Violet pressed Rita's hands between her own. "I make sure I move every day. Even if it's only jumping jacks in my room. I've noticed I feel better when I move."

Yet again, Rita's expression was doubtful.

"I write lists of all the things that are good."

Rita 's head tilted and she said quietly, "There are a lot of things that are good about Ham."

"Maybe write down every time you see him do something that is intended to make you happy or that shows his love?"

"He brought me a book," Rita said, "on the train. He'd read it, so he could talk to me about it when I took breaks from reading. He brought Father a special tobacco and a tin of biscuits to the landlady where his rooms are."

Violet nodded and waited.

"Denny wouldn't do that."

"He wouldn't."

"Jack would do it with calculation to deal with the earl."

"My father is very different from your father," Violet said.

"Being calculated is quite necessary with my father. Your father likes Ham, I think."

"Father told me it was hard to be in love. Especially after losing as we've lost."

Violet waited and let Rita pour over her thoughts. Finally Rita asked, "May I use some of your paper?"

With a nod, Violet got Rita a lap writing desk, a pen, and paper. As her friend started sketching out her thoughts, Violet left her in peace and took the bath James suggested. Jack must have mentioned at some point that Violet appreciated a bath when she was struggling. Or he was simply as clever at reading her as his son was.

She let the water rise over her head and listened to the echoing world around her. It was nearly silent, but the steaming water relaxed the muscles in her shoulders. Violet sat up slowly and then forced herself to reach for her toes and twist until the knots in her back started to release. As she relaxed back into the soothing water, Violet whispered to herself things to be thankful for and they all included ideas of how capable Ginny was.

Ginny was, Violet realized, going to be fine. She'd come home safe, of course she would. The worry in Violet's stomach eased and she felt a sudden need for a little something to eat and a nap to remedy the sleepless night.

CHAPTER 9

$\mathcal{V}$iolet would have liked to be there when Ginny and Geoffrey were caught by Smith. In her mind, Geoffrey tried to run and Smith tripped the lad, causing him to fall into quite an icy mud puddle. She suspected, however, that Geoffrey immediately gave up and sulked.

He was, she knew, a champion sulker. Lower lip just slightly out, a deliberately low mutter pitched too quietly to hear except the pitiable tone of his voice, the eyes that refused to meet anyone else's. He made you suffer along with him even if he was the one in the wrong and he knew it. Violet shook her head and wondered just what Smith would charge them for his help.

Violet thought she needed to add the payment to her will, with the instruction that Geoffrey was to pay it so that if she died before her younger brother, he would have that one final remembrance of the cost of his idiocy. No, she would change her will and leave a copy of it out where Lady

61

Eleanor would see it. Her stepmother would ensure Geoffrey knew, and Violet would be able to enjoy his reaction despite continuing to live.

Violet paced the parlor as she waited for the sound of the auto. Victor and Hargreaves had gone to get Ginny and the rest from the train. Violet had stayed behind, however, just to calm down. She'd become more tense after Beatrice let them know the children were caught, but this time it was from how she should react when she saw the two.

"You'll regret saying something terrible," Rita told Violet meaningfully before she glanced at Ham. "Just breathe. Maybe give them a dark look and leave. Something cryptic."

"I don't know," Denny said, "I wouldn't mind seeing Violet blow her top at the younglings. We'd get a flash of mother Vi."

"We've been getting flashes of mother Vi," Lila told him. "My lad, you are a bit dim sometimes. Violet panicking while the rest of us got another drink? It was Mama Vi come to play."

"Was it? You're a bit of a bear of a mum aren't you, Vi? Calm down, darling," Denny advised. "You'll turn that dark hair white before you're quite ready."

"No woman is ready for that," Rita shot out, rolling her eyes. She rose and poured a hefty glass of ginger wine, pressing it into Violet's hand. "It'll be all right, darling. Deep breaths and all that."

Violet shot them all dark looks and then suggested, "Why don't you all go to the devil?"

Ham's shout of laughter had everyone turning. "Not a bad plan. I could do with a cigar. Come along, Denny. Let's go find James and Rita's father."

Denny groaned and muttered, flinching when Violet shot

him another angry look. "Fine! Destroy my fun and all my dreams. They're in the library, Ham. It's where the older ones hide from us. Did you know James was thinking of writing a book? Don't ask him about it, for the love of heaven. Please."

"Come along, Mum," Rita said to Lila, taking both of Lila's hands and pulling her up. "Let's go find Kate and the babies, shall we? I hear little Agatha needs to spend more time with your tum to let the angel rub off on your mite."

"My mite is already an angel," Lila said lazily. She winked at Violet and let herself be tugged away, leaving Violet and Jack facing each other.

"What do I do?" Vi asked him. In the peace of just the two of them, she crossed to him, wrapped her arms around his waist, and told him. "I don't know what to do."

"I have no idea, darling." Jack rubbed his hand down her back. "Perhaps—" He trailed off and she could feel him move, guessing he was shaking his head.

"Am I overreacting?"

Jack laughed softly. "I think the term Mama Bear applies nicely to you, Vi. You're protective and caring and loving and you worry constantly about Ginny's happiness and safety. For that matter, Vivi and Agatha as well."

Violet bit her bottom lip and then admitted, "It's good I've known she was all right for a while. I suppose I did overreact."

Jack kissed her forehead. "I can understand Geoffrey wanting to hear from his first father about whatever nonsense your stepmother told him. I can imagine Ginny not wanting him to face that alone. I wish they would have just talked to us about it."

"They did hop trains."

"They did," Jack agreed carefully.

"That is stealing," Violet hissed, imagining Ginny missing her leap and getting hurt.

"It is," Jack said, but he couldn't quite hide the humor in his voice.

Violet carefully lifted her foot, stepped on his, and leaned her weight on him. He laughed aloud then, lifting her up by the waist with one arm.

"It is an adventure they will look back on and laugh over, Violet. Rather like this whole round of madness."

Violet pulled back, kicked him in the shin, and then when he dropped her, she pressed up and kissed him on the chin. "I suppose I'm a pendulum between worry and fear on the one side and amusement on the other."

"It is Christmas." Jack couldn't hide fighting his grin. He took her hand and pressed a kiss to her palm. "You could rage and punish and it wouldn't be a very Happy Christmas, would it? With Ginny, I wonder if a softer approach wouldn't work better. With Geoffrey? Darling, I think he might be immune to a woman's tirades."

"Did you just gently compare my reaction to how Lady Eleanor would react?"

"I was only suggesting that perhaps—" He snapped his mouth shut as she snatched her palm from his hand. Then his eyes widened in surprise when she took hold of his jacket and pulled him down to her, kissing him fervently.

Jack kissed her back, but when she dropped down from her toes, he asked, "What the devil?"

"Do you know it is my worst fear to be like Lady Eleanor? I have her and Aunt Agatha lumbering around in my head as examples of a mother, and—" Violet's eyes welled with tears and she admitted, "I might be exhausted with worry, furious that they scared me, and overreacting, but there is nothing I want less than to behave towards those I love as Lady Eleanor would."

Violet pressed her nose into Jack's chest and whispered, "This is why people have husbands and wives. To save each other from our missteps."

Jack laughed and tugged her down onto the sofa, relaxing when Vi relaxed. "What an adventurous holiday. What shall we do next Christmas to top this one, do you think? Rob a bank? Become wreckers and highwayman?"

"Get Ginny early from school and take her somewhere Geoffrey isn't?"

Jack snorted, and then he asked more seriously, "What do you wish to do?"

"Cuba again?"

"Ginny's holiday from school isn't that long."

Violet sighed and laid her head against his shoulder. Not that he could see it, but she hid away her wicked grin as she suggested, "Maybe Lady Eleanor would take Ginny for us."

Jack's pause and then shout of laughter was what welcomed Ginny home. She stepped through the doorway, her dark eyes wide with worry. If Geoffrey had arrived as well, he didn't follow Ginny into the parlor.

Violet and Ginny's gazes met, and Ginny's breathing increased. Violet stared at her ward and then was across the room, taking her by the face and examining her carefully. Vi noted the bruise on Ginny's chin, the dark circles under her eyes, and the pallor to her skin. Gently, Violet pressed a kiss on each side of Ginny's face, her forehead, and then the tip of her nose. The moment Vi let go of the cheeks, she squeezed Ginny tightly.

"I'm sorry," Ginny whispered.

Violet was shaking, hiding her emotions as she whispered back, "I'm glad you're all right, darling. I was so worried."

"I didn't think you would be," Ginny said, eyes tearing. "I thought it would be all right because you wouldn't worry."

Violet nibbled at the inside of her cheek and then told Ginny, "I must be failing you so terribly if you don't know how much we love you."

Tears fell then and Violet whispered, "Never mind, darling. Never mind. Shall we get you a hot bath and a hot meal and a long rest?"

Ginny curled into Violet's side, and Vi led her out of the parlor, glancing back at Jack, who nodded at her. "I'm sure Victor is seeing to Geoffrey in the way only a brother can."

Violet nodded and took Ginny upstairs, taking her to the bedroom Violet had picked out for her. The walls were a sunny yellow with cream and deeper gold accents. The bed looked like one a princess might sleep on and the walls were papered with yellow and gold paisley. Ginny's eyes widened and she whispered. "It's so lovely. Like for a princess."

"It was intended for Jack's sister."

Ginny knew that Jack didn't have one, so she started in surprise.

"She died when she was little. Jack's mother was so excited that after the baby was born, she started decorating, but when the little girl died, Jack's mother just shut the door. James suggested that you might enjoy the room."

"But—"

"It's been renewed," Violet told Ginny, ignoring the but. "New bedding and such, but I thought it would be nice if we kept a similar look. Especially since you have expressed no specific desires."

"Why?" Ginny's guilt as she took in the room and all its

meaning was enough for Violet to be done with her anger and worry.

Violet shook her head. You couldn't just explain loving someone. It took proof in the form of words and actions for it to be believed. And like Rita, sometimes it was hard to believe even then. Vi opened the door to Ginny's private bath and put the stopper into the drain. She turned the water on hot and gestured at Ginny.

"Our bags were stolen," Ginny muttered. "Neither of us have clothes."

Violet gestured to the bath and told Ginny, "I'll be back then."

Vi dug through her clothes until she found some looser dresses. Violet was slim while Ginny was taller and stronger. Vi opened the trunk in the closet and pulled out two of Ginny's presents and brought them to her in the bath. The bubbles and salts had mounded and Ginny seemed to be sleeping in the bath. Violet left her to it and rang the bell for one of the servants. A maid appeared and Violet requested a bowl of soup, bread, and tea to right Ginny.

Violet persuaded her ward from the bath, into the present of a pair of pajamas, and then a new kimono. "We'll visit the shops tomorrow before the new play and see what we can find. Were your uniforms in your trunk?"

Ginny nodded and Violet didn't let the rush of irritation show on her face.

"So we'll order those as well. I suppose you'll have to borrow until your new ones are available."

"I'm sorry," Ginny said.

Violet shook her head. "I'm glad you apologized. That said, you'd have needed new clothes anyway."

"I shouldn't have disappeared like that. We should have

been smarter about our things. We shouldn't have gone so long without contacting you and left you worrying. I'm sorry I didn't realize—"

Violet cupped Ginny's face and pressed a kiss against her forehead. "You are very young, my love, and it takes wisdom to recognize some of the consequences of our actions. Now you know that we do, in fact, love you. Along with love goes worry and care."

Ginny swallowed thickly.

"It's all right that you didn't know," Violet told her. "It has taken me quite a while to believe that anyone other than Victor would ever love me. Did you know? I thought that Victor had to love me because we were born together and I thought that my Aunt Agatha loved me because of her deathbed promise to my mother. I did believe that my mother loved me. It's like I can feel her at times. Like a flash of familiarity and my spirit tells me that Mother was near."

"Everyone loves you, Vi," Ginny told her, disbelieving.

Vi laughed in sheer mockery even though Ginny blushed. "That is not true, my love."

"Everyone I know tells me how lucky I am that you took me in."

"People comment on the things they don't understand all the time."

"But you took me in because I helped you with Isolde."

Violet paused to think and find the words. That had certainly been a part of it. Ginny's bravery had made it possible for Violet to find Isolde when she was at risk. It was an act that could never be repaid, but now—it didn't favor into Violet's feelings. They'd grown beyond debt and appreciation to something else.

"We wouldn't have known each other," Violet said, "if you hadn't helped me with Isolde."

Ginny waited, eyes fixed on Vi's face.

"That was why I looked after you while your grandmother was alive. The truth is—I've been so blessed by Aunt Agatha's fortune that I would probably look after any orphan that came into my life. You know—there were that family of orphans that Mrs. Lancaster took in. Jack and I could have done that, but Mrs. Lancaster was the one best suited to it. I wouldn't let her take you."

"Why?"

"I think," Violet said, "it's because I feel like we belong. The more I got to know you and the more I connected with you, it was like I was finding someone who had been missing. I hadn't known that you were missing until you were there and the hole in my heart was filled. If there is some design in our lives, Ginny, we were designed to be together."

"Do you really believe that?"

"Yes," Violet said firmly, meeting Ginny's gaze. "Yes, I absolutely believe it. I've never been one to fixate on blood making family. Even before my brothers died, I knew and loved Denny as my brother more than I knew and loved Peter and Lionel. I miss them and wish they hadn't died in the Great War, but—" Vi shook her head. It was complicated. Feelings were messy. They were messy and they didn't always add up the way that 'society' expected. What Violet knew was that Ginny matched Violet's heart and her life would never have been the same if something worse than losing luggage had happened while they were off on the hijinks-filled adventure. "I'm glad you're all right, but I think that's soup at the door, and I suggest you sleep off those dark circles under your eyes."

Ginny nodded obediently and as Violet situated the food with the girl and left the room, Ginny called, "I love you, Violet."

Vi's eyes were burning as she answered in a croak, "I love you too, Ginny." Vi could only hope that those five words somehow conveyed the ocean of feeling they were meant to illustrate.

CHAPTER 10

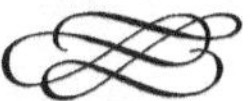

"It seems like taking a girl shopping for a whole new wardrobe isn't the best punishment. There should have been more tears," Rita told Violet as they got into the back of the auto with Ginny between them. "But that was delightful. I didn't expect there to be such lovely things or to have bought so much for myself."

"I suspect everything we just found was brought in the for the holiday," Violet said. "Perhaps we just made that shop woman's Christmas buying as much as we did. Think of it less as a reward, Rita, and more as a charitable endeavor for the village that I will be living in for the rest of my life."

"We didn't have to buy the whole shop," Ginny said. She stared at Violet, looking as though she had more to say. "Um—"

Violet glanced at the girl and then waited.

She blushed before she asked, "What is going to happen to Geoffrey?"

Violet shook her head. Geoffrey didn't want to go home,

but it wasn't really a decision that Violet and Victor could make for him when his mother demanded that he return. Gerald was a day behind the arrival of Ginny and Geoffrey— which would be something Violet would eventually endlessly point out. He was the only one, however, who might be able to talk to the earl, who could override his wife. Gerald may well have arrived while Violet and Ginny had been shopping. Nothing else would happen until Gerald had decided.

"Can you tell us what happened?" Rita asked softly.

Ginny shook her head, looking out the window. "I promised Geoffrey he could explain himself. It's all his—his —" Ginny stammered to a halt.

"That's fine then, isn't it?" Rita said easily, letting the poor girl off the hook. "I do like that blue dress on you, Ginny."

Ginny mumbled a thank you.

Violet grinned at Rita and then devilishly asked Ginny, "What do you think, Ginny my love? If a girl were to love a fellow who'd hurt her, how could she just let that go?"

Rita froze and Ginny swallowed thickly.

"I—Geoffrey and I—" Ginny blushed quite deeply and then muttered, "Well, he is a bit of a wart, isn't he? Only we started exchanging notes. Just jokes and such. You know? The only two our age in the families, we decided to be friends more out of self-defense, but our friendship grew from there."

"Violet told me to write, too," Rita grumbled.

"Vi told me that there's a magic in writing. It turned Geoffrey from wart to someone I understood better."

Rita swallowed thickly but nodded. "You owe me quite a delightful present, Violet, throwing my secrets out like that, but Ginny is a smart one, isn't she?"

"I thought you could use some cleverness and Ginny has

it to spare. Your problem is that you've asked me what to do. You should have known better. What do I know?"

Rita laughed darkly and said, "Father told me to suck it up. In fact, this morning he told me he quite liked James and was prepared to have him be fellow grandfathers as James looked upon Ham as a son. I feel pressured from all sides." Rita's disgust was enough to have her scowling. She leaned forward with a gasp. "Hargreaves, my favorite fellow, would you please stop here?"

Calmly, Hargreaves moved to the side of the street and pulled the auto off the road.

"Just a mo'," Rita said, jumping out of the auto. She returned in a few minutes with two stacks of paper in a brown paper bag. One stack was pink, the other blue.

"What's all this?" Violet asked, her smile barely disguised.

"Oh shut your mouth," Rita said. "Paper, a journal, a pretty pen. What more do you want from me?"

"Praise," Violet shot back immediately, winking at Ginny.

Ginny giggled and Violet leaned back with delight.

"I might despise you a little," Rita muttered.

"You love me," Violet said as Hargreaves pulled back onto High Street and then towards Violet's home. "Are we ready for this play tonight, ladies?"

"Are you ready?" Rita shot back. Her gaze promised revenge as she glanced at Ginny. "Did you know Father Christmas has quite an eager eye for our Vi?"

Ginny's mouth dropped.

"I understand he has decided to add Violet to his slew of lovers."

Ginny gasped. "You're bamming me."

"Never," Rita swore, crossing her finger over her heart. "Never would I do such a thing."

Violet shook her head. "Rita, did you want to join with me in explaining to Ginny about the birds and the bees?"

Ginny gasped again, shaking her head frantically.

"Oh, would I?" Rita rubbed her hands together in glee. "Shall we have a private tea then? A private tea, a private talk?"

"No," Ginny said. "I know about…. actions."

"But it's about more than that, isn't it? It's about choices and times and seasons and—"

"Oh please stop," Ginny moaned. "I'm quite uncomfortable."

"You do realize that Victor and Isolde both rushed down the aisle, don't you?"

Ginny was blushing brilliantly as she nodded. Her entire face, which was normally even-colored, was a burning red. Her gaze was fixed on the floor, and she was fighting the need to cover her ears, her hands half-going to her ears and then back to her lap again as she failed to hide her embarrassment.

"You know," Violet mused evilly, "I was going to talk to you about this before you left me worried, but now I'm going to enjoy your misery as we discuss the act, the fluids, the whatnots."

"Oh…my…bloody…hell," Ginny breathed in panic.

"Tell me," Rita asked with glee, "when do you know the time is right?"

Ginny started to answer, met Hargreaves's impervious gaze in the rear-view mirror and shuddered, crossing her arms over her chest.

"We've arrived, madam," Hargreaves told Violet, not quite able to hold back the twitch of his lips.

"Wonderful," Violet said, winking at him as Ginny leapt

out of the auto and raced inside. Violet called after, "I'll see you in my sitting room at teatime, darling Ginny."

She squawked and ran up the stairs.

Rita laughed in answer and then told Violet, "My goodness, I think I forgive you."

"See, it's not that hard." She saw Ham leave the house at the same time that Rita did. Rita hesitated, then lifted her chin and continued toward the house. Violet hooked her arm through Hargreaves's, holding him back. Ham walked down the steps to Rita and spoke, though too quietly for Violet to hear. Rita started to answer, paused, and then took his arm. Ham glanced at Vi with a look that could only be called pleased. Violet nodded at him once, not bothering to hide her smile, then nudged Hargreaves towards the door. His low laugh couldn't be hidden by an impervious expression when she had her hand on his arm.

"Hargreaves," Violet told him brightly, "I do hope you're having a Happy Christmas."

"Indeed, I am, madam."

"It just warms the cockles of one's heart, doesn't it? To have our Ginny back, to see those two trotting about the wood as they should."

"If I may say, Mrs. Vi," Hargreaves told her, "it's seeing you all together and happy that warms my heart."

"You may," Violet joked as Hargreaves opened the door and gestured her inside. Violet choked on her laughter as one of the pug pups squatted down and piddled in the hall. She pasted a dark look on her face and called, "Gerald! Your dog! My heavens, man, soiling my house!"

Hargreaves didn't bother to hide his laugh as Violet picked up the puppy and nuzzled faces. Her older brother appeared in the doorway.

"Violet Wakefield," he declared. "You are a devil! A devil! Bloody hell! You knew exactly what you were doing when you handed Lottie those puppies, let her fall in love with one nuzzle, and then set us on the train."

Vi widened her eyes and glanced innocently at Hargreaves. "Whatever does he mean?"

Gerald growled, took the puppy, and then muttered an apology to Hargreaves as he left the mess. Vi grinned. "I'll get it, shall I? I believe I might have engineered that. Just a little."

"A bit really."

"A smidgeon. Barely any at all."

Hargreaves shook his head and said, "Mrs. Vi, I will be dealing with the mess. Off with you."

"Tell the staff there will be extra bonuses for all the puppy messes."

"That is why we're paid, Mrs. Vi."

Violet disappeared into the parlor, leaving her cloche and coat. Ginny wasn't about, but Geoffrey was. Violet crossed to him, took his face between her hands, and squeezed his cheeks as if he were a babe. "You know, darling," Violet told him idly, "if you determine to go it alone, you'll find that we hunt you down and drag you home."

Geoffrey tried to look away, but Violet held his face tighter. "I did miss you, lovey."

He didn't answer, but he did back up rather quickly. She lifted a brow at Victor, noted his tight mouth and then glanced at Jack who shook his head lightly.

"Tell me."

"My mother said that she didn't marry my father because he was stepping out on her with some longtime lover. Complete with children."

Vi paused, noting the look on his face.

"Real siblings, you know?"

Violet did not nod. She knew about siblings who you weren't raised with but came to love. She knew about siblings you were raised with and their special bond. She knew that family was made of endless variations, and she knew the loss you felt when you were the sibling who was left out.

"I understand," she said softly.

"I wanted to talk to him. To ask him if that's why they didn't marry. I wanted to...to...see if there were siblings and such. She talks about them as though they were the bastards. The dirty ones. It's not just them, though, is it? I'm just as much of a bastard as they are."

Violet reached out and took his hand, but he shrugged her off.

"What did you find?"

"Find? She lied. She always does, doesn't she? She took the truth and swirled it up. The moment your father came trotting around and eyeing her, she threw my father over. The mistress came after, but she did come. There are four boys who look just like me. Mother makes it seem like they stole her life, but they didn't. She's not the victim. She never is outside of her own head."

Violet bit down on her bottom lip.

"I can't deal with her."

"You don't have to," Violet told him.

"She demands that I come home. Gerald says I have to deal with her."

"I will," Violet told Geoffrey and his gaze looked up in shock. "Let me be clear, she is your mother, and even in all the ways I disagree with her, there is no doubt that she adores you."

"She lied to me!"

"She painted you a picture that made you think she was the heroine because she wants to matter to you."

Geoffrey cursed and Gerald reached over and smacked the back of his head.

"You have a father," Violet said calmly, "and it isn't Mr. Fitzhugh. It's Henry Carlyle. He knew you weren't his, and he didn't treat you any differently. If anything, you got a bit more attention."

"Maybe because he was considering throwing me to the gutter."

"Maybe it was because he wanted to be sure he did as good of a job with you as he did with us, and he did better because he was paying attention. I will tell you the same thing I've already said once this holiday. You can tell if someone loves you by how they behave. Your mother suffocates you with her love. Your father—the earl—loves you by ensuring you're treated just the same as the rest of us. Gerald loves you with his smacks. Victor and I with sarcasm and attention. Ginny with the way she went with you and didn't leave you alone."

Geoffrey's nearly albino complexion had flared almost as red as Ginny when Violet had brought up making love. "And you can be sure I love you with the telephone call I am about to make. Go, get a suit from Victor, love on the babies, and prepare yourself for a village play that will be remembered through the ages."

CHAPTER 11

*V*iolet dressed for the play carefully. She'd considered an evening gown and then imagined the evening-out wear for their small village. She changed her choice to a garnet red dress she'd wear to church with a shorter strand of pearls, a cameo broach on her chest, and a pair of black satin gloves. This time, if Father Christmas should catch her, he wouldn't molest her wrist.

"Jack," Violet told him as he leaned down to kiss her neck, "you look smashing."

He grinned at her in the mirror. "You look like a housewife for the small town."

She reached up to his neck, found a hair that wasn't slicked down, and tugged it. His laugh rang in her ear and she got up. His arm was around her waist, so she turned and found herself pressed against him from chest to thigh.

"Well, hello there, Mrs. Wakefield," he said and kissed her neck just above her pearls.

"Mr. Wakefield," she said starchily. "If I'm going to be a

village housewife, you had better watch yourself, sirrah. There's a rogue Father Christmas looking to find all the naughty wives around."

Jack laughed into her neck and then shook his head. "I confess, I do not understand it."

"It's the neglect," Violet announced as though she knew. "These fellows these days, laddie. Catching themselves a lass, bringing her home, and demanding love while they skip out to the pub with the boys. Then along comes suave grandfather with a dimple, compliments, and a turn of phrase."

"Dimples?" Jack asked. "Is that what you want?"

"I prefer a broad set of shoulders," she told him. "A strong arm." She paused tellingly and then gave him a grave expression as she added, "Uninjured."

"Volley across the port bow, Captain," Jack told her, kissing her neck again. "I don't know. There's little trouble to capture you with just the one arm."

"Well, you know, you would pretend."

"Would I?" he asked and then lifted her up. "Why are we going to this again?"

"To give the money to the charity in front of Cowell."

"Ah—"

Violet shook her head before he could comment and added, "To see the fabulous Mrs. Cowell."

"Ahhhh." Jack grinned and squeezed her tight enough she oomphed.

"To discover the brilliance of the good mayor."

He snorted at that.

"To torture Gerald."

"Now we have it," Jack said.

"Perhaps a little, but mostly—" She paused and waited, and Jack kissed her one more time and then let her slide down his body and onto her feet. She stepped back, smoothed her hair, and then added with emphasis, "Because your father said we had to."

Jack's shout of laughter chased her out the door and Violet found Kate in a nearly matching dress, pale and tired-looking. Violet stared as Kate placed a hand to her chest, hiccupped, and then moaned a little.

"By Jove, woman! Are you with child again?"

Kate moaned.

"I cannot begin to imagine what you were thinking. Though that might have been the problem. Do we need to have the talk?"

A rather astonishing burp echoed in the hall and Kate gasped. "I don't know if I can go tonight."

"What do you need?"

"Make Victor go away?" Kate's eyes filled with tears as she added, "He keeps apologizing as if I weren't there."

"Do you need another copy of the book?"

Kate tucked her arms close and admitted, "Nothing has been right since the babies were born. I—I—I never even started again. I only realized what was happening because I was so sick."

Violet winced and then added, "Darling, you need to use more than just your schedule."

"Obviously," Kate wailed. "But here we are."

"You can do it."

"You haven't shot one out, have you? My lady bits aren't back to normal and here comes another! And I don't feel good. Dear Agatha has noticed and gives me the most woebegone eyes. And Vivi, she just rejects me now, doesn't she? Chooses the nanny or Victor. It's entirely unfair, I tell you."

Violet opened her arms, and Kate scoffed and snapped, "Hugging makes me want to sick up. Breathing makes me want to sick up. I'm not going. I don't want to see this stupid Father Christmas or the play and you can be sure I don't want to lie with a smile and pretend to be quite happy. I—" Kate stared at Violet in horror, started to cry, and muttered, "By heaven, I've gone mad. Stark, raving, lock-her-in-Bedlam-bonkers."

Violet bit down on her bottom lip before she said the wrong thing again.

"You know the worst part?" Kate hissed.

Violet shook her head helplessly.

"Lila. Glowing. Never sicking up. Not once. I might hate her."

Violet started to ask who could blame Kate for that, but Vi was quite afraid to do such a thing.

"Never again," Kate swore, then put her hand over her mouth and darted into the bedroom across from Vi's.

"Bloody hell," Violet muttered, staring after her sister-in-law.

Jack dared to put his head out of the door into the hall. He breathed a curse. Their gazes met and Violet pressed her hand over her mouth.

"She has gone mad, hasn't she?" Jack whispered, darting a glance towards the closed door and then back at Vi with horrified eyes.

"She doesn't feel well," Violet whispered back. "To be honest, she scares me."

"Me too," Jack said without a bit of sarcasm.

Violet took Jack's arm and they went down the stairs. Victor hadn't arrived, but everyone else was dressed at varying levels. Rita wore something that edged more towards an evening gown while Lila looked ready for an afternoon tea. Denny was wearing what looked more like a morning suit that was a bit snug, and Ham wore his usual—though a newer version—of his dark brown suit, yellow shirt, and brown and yellow plaid tie. Gerald wore a black suit while Lottie wore a respectable rose dress that would blend into a nice restaurant or a church afternoon.

"Don't you all look interesting," Violet said, grinning at the differences.

James and Frederick Russell snorted.

"Where are Smith and Beatrice?"

"It seems Smith extorted dinner and a walk from Beatrice. They went to a little restaurant, but Beatrice said they intended to see the play," Lottie answered with a wide grin.

Gerald tugged one of her long curls and added, "Smith heard about your conquest and wanted to see it for himself."

"That sounds more likely," Denny said, rubbing his hands together. "He's not the only one. I see you look ready for church," Denny told Violet, elbowing Ham. "We were making bets about how you would turn out, and I laid my wager on a bit of a posh garden tea, but you know—warmer."

"I think you've won," Gerald grumbled. "How is that?"

"You might be the brother," Lila told him, "but Denny and I have lived in Violet's pocket since we were in school. Denny—if he had a scrap of talent—could have drawn how she'd look."

"It's as though we've never gone to a village fest," Violet muttered and shook her head at them. "We look as though we've all dressed for a different event."

"I would have dressed correctly," Rita said, glancing at the others, "if I had known we were going to a village play."

Violet laughed and then glanced towards the stairs.

Victor and Ginny came down and Violet lifted a brow at her brother. He met her gaze, flushed, and then glanced behind him. No one, however, appeared. He turned from the stairs, cast her a pleading look, and Violet nodded slightly.

"Kate has decided to play with the babies instead of the locals," Violet lied easily. "Who is ready?"

VIOLET SPIED Joan Oates the second that she stepped through the door. The woman sat in the back row and was knitting away despite the open seats at the front. Next to Joan was a woman who had the same wicked gaze and then two younger girls who carried on with the same wittiness of expression. Violet crossed to them, bypassing without regret where the mayor stood waving at her.

"Hullo, hullo!" Violet said with a grin. "How delightful!"

"Oh, Mrs. Wakefield," the mayor said, calling Vi's attention despite her sidestepping him. "I have reserved your party seats at the front."

Denny waggled his brows behind the back of the mayor and one of the mayor's daughters snorted.

"What an idiot," his daughter hissed. "He's blind to anything but his own teeth in the glass."

"Shush," the younger version of Joan Oates hissed. "Put a smile on your face, pretend to enjoy yourself. Think dark thoughts if you must—"

"I must," one of the girls whispered back.

"But keep them to yourself," her mother snapped.

Violet had to bite down on the inside of her cheek to hide the laugh.

"Just up here," the mayor told Violet, holding out his hand

to take hers.

"We've decided to sit here in the back."

"But you won't be able to see me there." His confused expression was just ridiculous.

Violet took in a deep breath. Denny giggled low and then said loudly, "Violet is a bit of a theater connoisseur. You can see the whole stage better in the back, you know. A bit like box seats."

"Oh, but—" The mayor tried to hold out his hand to Violet again. "No, no."

"Yes," Victor snapped. He hadn't lost the worried expression about Kate, and he wasn't feeling charitable. "Off with you, man. Violet likes your mother-in-law, and we'd prefer to be a bit farther back."

The mayor blushed and then nodded. Violet took the free seat next to Joan Oates and said, "Happy Christmas, darling. Have you made all the puddings and whatnots? Only a few more days—"

"I have," Joan replied. "This is my daughter, Shari. And my treasures, Ruby and Rachel."

Violet winked at the girls and introduced her party.

"Oh there are a lot of you," Ruby said. She glanced at her mother and then gestured to the seats next to herself and her sister for Ginny and Geoffrey, who escaped the others happily.

Ginny had a low-level blush since the discussion about relations between men and woman that Rita and Violet had forced on the girl during tea. She hadn't, in fact, appeared at dinner at all, and Rita had cackled when one of the housemaids said that Ginny wasn't feeling well.

The play was—to be plain—awful. Nearly every scene had some man fawning over Father Christmas, praising him with illogical lines. Two of the poor women who were playacting waited for laughter as they'd clearly been directed, only no one laughed, barring Denny who did—in fact—laugh enough for most of the crowd.

As the players took the stage the final time and bowed, Denny jumped to his feet, clapping loudly. He got several startled looks before one-by-one others reluctantly followed suit.

Ruby leaned towards Violet and asked, "Is your friend making fun of my dad?"

Violet hesitated to answer, but the girl's mother muttered, "Of course he is, Ruby. Your father is a self-indulged peacock in a flock of serviceable guinea fowl. The contrast has given him a level of pride he doesn't deserve."

"It's all right, darling," Joan told her daughter, shooting Violet an agonized look.

"Did you see him? By heaven, Mother! The way he trailed his hand over Harriet Piggott's neck? He used that little move with me when he was aiming to destroy my life. Flashing that dimple. He probably uses the same stupid lines on her as he does on me."

Violet shot Geoffrey a look, which he understood at once, and he rose from his seat. "Would you like to take a walk with Ginny and me? Ruby? Rachel? It would be fun to learn about the area. We're so new, you know."

Both girls got up gratefully, and Joan's daughter shuddered. "I shouldn't have said that in front of them."

"They have eyes and wits, thank heaven," Joan told her daughter unsympathetically. "They know what he is."

"A fool."

"And a thief," someone hissed.

They all turned, but whoever said it had disappeared back

into the crowd leaving the building.

"A thief?" Violet asked.

Joan's mouth was snapped together tightly and she refused to answer. Jack rose then and pulled Violet up.

"What an adventure," Jack said charitably. "Lovely to see you again, Mrs. Oates. So nice to meet you, Mrs. Cowell."

They nodded and James turned around and whispered low. "Mingle."

"I don't want to," Denny said.

"Mingle!" James ordered again low. "Put a smile on your face. Compliment little girls' dresses. Comment on the decorations and look pleased."

"Oh I am pleased," Denny said.

"Don't stick together," James snapped. "Spread out. Quarter hour. Go."

Ham held out his arm to Rita, and Violet caught the sight of the purple paper she'd seen earlier that day in Rita's bag. A letter had been written, Violet thought, and Ham had tucked it into his coat. What did it say?

James set the first example and stepped away, bringing along Frederick Russell.

Violet took Jack's arm, and he led her over to a man of a similar age. She had lost sight of her favorite in Joan Oates, but the old friend of Jack was married to a woman called Leta who had not accompanied the mayor, so Violet automatically appreciated her.

"So nice to meet you," Violet said. "It's so fun to see those who knew Jack when he was a sprightly fellow."

"Oh I don't think Jack was every sprightly," the man laughed, nudging Jack with his elbow. He patted his own slightly pudgy stomach and added, "Not that I qualify anymore either."

"He used to be the stringiest bean you'd ever seen, Vi."

Violet laughed, as did Leta who seemed unbothered by the change in her husband. Before the women could answer, there was a horrified scream at the back of the stage.

"Was that Ginny?" Violet asked, glancing frantically around. She felt Jack take her wrist.

Another scream. This one not Ginny. Violet's gaze darted about the room, looking for Ginny.

"It's Father!" the voice screamed. "It's Father!"

Ham grabbed Jack's arm, tugging him towards the stage and the area behind it just as Rita took Violet's hand.

"Was that Ginny?"

"I think so," Rita said.

Violet started for her girl, but Rita held Violet back, shaking her head. "You don't need to see whatever it is."

"What is it?" Leta asked.

"Our Ginny isn't one to scream over a stumble," Rita told Leta.

"What does that mean?" Jack's friend asked.

"Nothing good," Violet said direly, her gaze fixed on the stage until Ginny stepped out. Before Violet could reach her, Victor did. He held his hands up and Ginny let him lift her off the stage. A moment later, Geoffrey followed, white as a sheet.

He jumped down next to Ginny and crossed to Violet. It took Geoffrey several attempts before he said, "It's Father Christmas."

"The mayor?" Leta asked.

Geoffrey nodded, swallowing thickly. "He's dead."

"He was stabbed," Ginny said a moment later, "in the back."

CHAPTER 12

Violet wrapped her arm around Ginny and looked at Geoffrey. She'd always thought he was too pale. After seeing a dead man? He was ghostly. She glanced at Rita and their gazes met with the same thought: 'Here we go again.'

The cycle of coming across a death and being sucked into the lives around that death was starting again. Violet supposed part of this curse had to be that Jack was such a well-known investigator, and she had concluded that she just had the worst luck. She and her friends had been touched by the personification of death or some other such madness.

It wasn't only that. She was a meddler. She dove into other people's business even when there wasn't murder on the line. She was easy to talk to and unexpected in her thoughts and actions. With an exceptional ability to pick at the threads of people's lives, she could understand what motivated them. Perhaps that came from being raised by a woman who was brilliant. Perhaps Violet was looking for an excuse to learn the details of people's lives. Her specialty seemed to be gossip, quiet conversations, and mean asides.

Jack shot her a commanding look that she already intended to ignore and then he leapt onto the stage. Vi's twin said something and Jack looked around the theater before nodding and replying. A moment later, both of her favorite men were out of her sight.

The room wasn't a traditional theater. It was a gathering hall used by the town for things like dances, fundraisers, and meetings with a stage at one end for whatever purpose could be imagined.

Violet's friends had been somewhat scattered around the room while Violet and Jack had been visiting with the locals, and they were gathering as if drawn together.

Denny and Lila approached first, took in the sight of the upset children, and still Denny's glee didn't fade.

"Hargreaves and Jack's man should be here with the autos," Rita pointed out. "Perhaps we should get the children home and send them back for Jack and Ham."

"No," Ginny said, suddenly going from a shuddering mess to demanding. "No. We can't just leave the Cowell girls. They might need help."

Violet closed her eyes and breathed in. The panic in Ginny's gaze was setting off Violet's own reaction to a death. She was becoming numb to it, but the numbness too often equaled a malaise that was difficult to shake. Violet tucked Ginny's arm through her own, keeping their hands clasped, so Vi could comfort and also keep a finger on Ginny's trembling.

"I'm not sure we're the best to help the Cowell ladies," Violet told Ginny gently. "We have only just met them."

"He couldn't have been stabbed," Leta suddenly said,

glancing between Ginny and Violet. Her expression seemed to demand that Ginny admit she lied. "He looked all right for an older man, but surely it was a heart attack."

"He was stabbed," Ginny said again. Her precise tone was almost too cool for the comfort of anyone who might have a more giving heart.

"How would you know?" Leta's husband asked lightly. "You're just a child."

"He's not my first stabbing," Ginny muttered, and Violet gasped along with the rest of the circle. "However, the pool of blood under his body, the wound on his back, the lack of a gunshot—those are all obvious reasons why he was stabbed. You don't just have a pool of blood under you if your heart attacked you or if you had an apoplectic fit."

Leta turned paler than Geoffrey and her husband shot Violet a dark look.

Violet closed her eyes and told Leta, "That wasn't us. The other stabbing." Vi paused, because her mind was scattered at the idea of yet another body, and she focused on Ginny. "Was it?"

Ginny shook her head. "My uncle was stabbed before my parents died, but we found his body. Father took us looking for him when he didn't come home after work. We were worried and no one really thought that he'd be dead. I saw him first. I saw it all."

"He was?" Violet gasped. "You did?"

"They'd tossed him in an alley. I noticed his hand sticking out from the trash they threw over him. Father didn't think he was dead, so he kept on going."

Leta shuddered, pale and horrified.

"Uncle's killers took the weapon as well. Wound on the

back, pool of blood, too pale. That pained surprised look. It was all the same as Father Christmas."

Geoffrey glanced at Vi, saw her shock, and added, "Robbed for his paycheck and dumped in an alley."

"You know?" Rita demanded. "Why do you know about Ginny's secrets?"

"They write to each other," Violet told Rita, lifting her brows and then feeling immediately guilty for making a joke when someone had just died.

"Oh my, well—" Leta glanced at all of them and then muttered, "Let's go, honey. I don't feel so well."

Violet watched them leave and Denny stage-whispered, "We're too much for them."

"We're too much for ourselves." Violet pulled away from Ginny. "You're both shaking and matter-of-fact. It's a conundrum. Darling, are you all right?"

Ginny considered for a moment and then shook her head. "No, I don't think so. I feel quite ill."

"Let's get you home."

"No," Ginny snapped. "We can't just leave the Cowell girls. They said that no one liked their mother or grandmother because of their father. If we leave them, people might not step in and help."

Violet glanced at Rita who shrugged. "I suppose I could reach out."

"They don't know you. They barely know Violet or I, but at least we had a few minutes to speak before he died. It had better be us." Ginny ran her hands over her arms and she eyed Geoffrey as though she wanted to jump right into those slender arms but knew she couldn't.

"Ginny—" Vi started.

"We can't leave," Ginny said. "Ruby and Rachel just saw

their father dead on the ground. They need someone. I cried for days over my uncle, and he was mean as a snake."

Violet pressed a kiss on Ginny's forehead and tucked her closer. "Fine. Of course. We'll try to help."

Rita added, "We do have the two autos. We could take the Cowell women home. Make sure they have everything they need. Give them time to recover together in their home."

"What could we give them that would help?" Geoffrey asked, leaning over to breathe with his hands on his legs. Rita rubbed his back as Ginny shuddered again. "What they need is their father."

There was enough emphasis in that statement that Violet suspected Geoffrey was speaking from his own heart. Did he mean the earl? Or his first father?

"They need him not to be gone. To be theirs still."

The earl, Violet thought, and once again, she adjusted what she was going to say to her father when she telephoned.

"Of course," Violet said, but she doubted of all people there, any of them would be comforting to the family. Surely some friend of the family would help. To make Ginny happy, however, they could remain until the Cowell women were able to go home.

Violet and the others waited until Jack appeared with one of the constables. Jack pulled Violet to the side and said low, "He was stabbed, and we're officially assigned to the case. I'm sorry that we're involved, Violet."

Vi nodded. "Ginny wants to make sure that the Cowell women get home all right. She's worried."

"She has good instincts. The girls are hysterical. Their mother and grandmother have them in a small room. Every time we check on them, we find those girls wailing. I think they might need—I don't know. A slap? Smelling salts? They need something more than the women seem to be providing, but Mrs. Cowell won't let the doctor see them."

"Why?" Violet hissed.

"Her husband had an affair with the doctor's wife."

"No!"

Jack nodded, jaw tight. The muscle was flexing and his eyes were furious. "Mrs. Cowell is not a woman who is blind to her husband's faults. When I asked her why she wouldn't let the doctor in, she told me as calmly as if she were mentioning the weather. 'I'm sorry, Dr. Black cannot see my girls. I wouldn't feel comfortable with that seeing as how he hated my husband, may well have killed him, and currently wonders if my daughters are the siblings of his youngest.'"

"She said that?"

"Same tone you'd use for saying, 'So much rain lately.'"

"Do you think that she's right about her husband?"

"I asked her what she thought," Jack said quietly. "She said all three girls have the same deep dimples as Cowell."

"If Mrs. Cowell is like her mother, she's not an idiot. She's probably right." Violet rubbed the back of her neck. "I would know if you were stepping out on me. Not that women who don't realize are dim, I just don't think he was trying all that hard to hide his behavior. If I ever see a child with penetrating eyes and a strong jawline and that child is not mine, I will murder you. Just so we're clear."

"Clearly," Jack said blandly. He paused for a moment and took her face between his hands. "I would know if you stepped out on me as well, Violet. It wouldn't be you I murdered."

She kissed his palm and then said, "Be safe."

"Victor is helping the constable make notes about who was here and where they were. Max Cowell died between the curtain dropping and when we heard the scream. It wasn't even twenty minutes, I don't think."

Violet bit her lip. "The Cowell women and Joan had all disappeared from the room by then."

Jack nodded. "We haven't been able to discuss it with them."

"We could ask if the girls stayed with Ginny and Geoffrey for the entire time."

Jack sighed. "There's no way to keep you fully out of it, is there?"

"I'll stay out of it, Jack, but I think we both know that I'll have a much better chance getting some of the town women to speak to me."

"Do you think a woman killed him?" he asked and then admitted, "It's possible. There's the money side of things. Ham and I need to track that down. There's the chance of the killer being his wife or his mother-in-law or one of his daughters. One of the husbands of his lovers. The number of suspects is rather alarming really."

"You'll be able to narrow it down," Violet said, squeezing his hand. "That window of time will make it easier."

Violet glanced around the theater area they'd had yet to leave. Gerald and Lottie were sitting in the back row of seats, Lottie's head on Gerald's shoulder. Lila was sitting next to them. Geoffrey had taken a seat in front of Gerald but three rows up. Violet wasn't surprised Denny wasn't sitting when there was gossip to be found. Denny had wandered away when there was nothing good to learn from Violet and Ginny.

Vi caught sight of Victor entering the room, tapping someone on the shoulder, and taking them out. Had Violet entirely missed when they were telling them stay in the room? Or perhaps constables were just blocking the exit? Violet noticed several small groups of families or friends around the large room. Now that she was paying attention, she noted them glancing over their shoulders towards the stage.

The reason, Vi thought, that no announcement had been made about staying was that very few people were trying to leave. Anyone who hadn't left immediately after the play was still in the room. They were lingering on purpose. There was the woman whose hair he had tugged at her house. It was the intimate move one didn't realize conveyed quite so much. Letting a stray hair curl around your finger meant that there had been a time when his fingers were dug into that head of hair. A man laughed deeply and then tried to cover his amusement. Laughing while a family was dealing with their father's death was in poor taste, but Violet wondered who had remained because they loved the mayor.

CHAPTER 13

Violet knocked on the door where the Cowell woman and Mrs. Oates were staying. Mrs. Oates opened the door, frowned at Violet, and then looked past her as if checking to see who came with her.

"We have an auto," Violet said, "and would be happy to have you driven home."

Mrs. Oates glanced behind her and Violet noticed Ruby sitting in the chair next to her mother curled down onto her lap. Rachel was lying against Mrs. Cowell's shoulder with her mother's arm wrapped around her shoulders.

Violet winced and then met Mrs. Cowell's eyes. "There are still quite a few people here, but Jack says that there is a door in the back and Hargreaves can pull the auto up to just by the alley, so you can have some privacy."

Mrs. Oates's frown deepened and she hesitated. "I think Shari should walk out, head up, shoulders straight, but the girls—"

"It might be easier for them to not have to pretend,"

Violet suggested softly. "Either way, our man would be happy to drive you."

"I suppose it would be easier to just accept a ride," Mrs. Oates said. "Someone will be well-meaning and ill-advised."

Violet bit back an insistence that walking home would be ill-advised indeed.

Instead she asked again, "After Hargreaves gets you home, is there anything you or your daughter needs?"

Mrs. Oates snorted meanly and whispered low and carefully, "A better husband and father who didn't die? I'm not sure that they didn't get just what they needed when someone stabbed him. It was an act of generosity, and I don't care how cold that makes me seem. Max Cowell was a worthless piece of human flesh, and the world is a better place."

Violet couldn't help but glance towards Mrs. Oates's granddaughters, but there was no reaction. Since there was no reaction, Violet bit her bottom lip, but pulled Mrs. Oates from the room.

"He was murdered," Violet told the woman.

She stared at Violet as if to ask why she was bothering to explain the sun came up daily.

"Who do you think did it?"

Mrs. Oates eyed Violet sideways. "Pick someone. It could have been them. The Creek family who was being robbed of their charitable donations? The town elders who are going to find out eventually that the bakery has been doing worse and yet the Cowell house continued to be improved? The husbands of the wives who strayed in heart if not in mind? The list is endless."

Violet hissed and then asked, "If you were to lay a wager?"

"I wouldn't bother wasting any more of my time and

effort on him. What he'll get from me is a glossed over history for his daughters, and he doesn't deserve that much. He was a mistake in every way except for with the arrival of my granddaughters."

Violet nodded. "Hargreaves is waiting with the auto. We'll bring over a care basket in the morning."

Mrs. Oates frowned and then took hold of a cane that Violet hadn't seen the day of the mayor's visit. The poor woman must have been feeling her age at the thought of witnessing her son-in-law's spectacle of a play. Violet took hold of the door and re-opened it for Mrs. Oates so she didn't have to handle both the cane and the door.

With a sigh, Violet turned back to Jack, walking towards him until he was near enough to lift his brows in question. Had she learned anything? Vi shook her head in answer. He tucked her into his side since there was no one about, pressing his chin on the top of her head, and they breathed each other in. Violet had learned in the spew of murders in her life that it was important to take a few moments to curl into the people you loved and count your blessings.

In fact, she'd learned that in her day-to-day. Take time to write about the things you had been given, the things that really matter. Vivi and Agatha being healthy. Jack recovering from his wound. Loving and being loved.

Violet pulled back and pushed up on her toes, getting a kiss on his chin before she dropped back down to the ground. "Kate is expecting."

"I wondered, since she has disappeared into her bedroom."

"Victor looks guilty, doesn't he?"

Jack's shout of laughter was ill-timed when Mrs. Oates opened the door for her daughter and granddaughters. Vi and Jack winced in unison, snapping their mouths closed. They took a step back, but Violet took hold of Jack's hand. She wasn't going to apologize for taking a moment with her husband.

They might not know it, but Violet knew too well that Jack would be mostly gone until the case was over. He'd find out who the town elders were, who was taking the contributions, where the money went, who were the mayor's lovers, who had alibis. He'd put it all together, and in the end—he'd find the killer.

That meant, however, when Violet sat down with Kate to play Christmas carols and sing with their friends, Jack might not be there. It meant that when they added peppermint to their cocoa, he wouldn't be there. He'd miss building the gingerbread house and all the little things they did.

Violet sighed. He caught her sigh, and he knew her well enough to guess what was bothering her. He took her face between his hands the moment the last of the victim's family slipped through the door and kissed her soundly.

"I love you, Violet Wakefield."

She pressed her face into his chest and caught her breath before she answered, "And I love you."

"Go home, Vi."

She nodded against his chest. Evening had fallen before the play had started, and night was well and truly present. She needed to telephone her father in the morning, talk to Geoffrey and Ginny about what they'd seen, and see what she could discover from Oakes and the Cowell women. It wasn't lost on Violet that they were—all of them—suspects.

Jack hadn't been able to get information from the women, but Violet thought she might get some answers. Even if there were just a few.

"FATHER," Violet said, hating the tinny sound of her voice traveling.

There was a long pause before she heard him clear his throat and reply, "Violet, are you letting me know which train to expect Gerald and Geoffrey on?"

"Geoffrey doesn't want to come home, Father. He wants to stay here."

She waited for her voice to travel the line and wondered how he would react. Would he feel slighted because the son he'd claimed was rejecting him? Would he understand? Would he reject Geoffrey back?

"What am I supposed to do about that, Vi?"

"Father, I think you need to get on the train and come here and tell him that if he doesn't want to come to you, you'll come to him."

"Victor made it clear Ellie wasn't welcome, Vi."

"Father, you are neither blind nor dumb, so please don't play stupid with me."

His laugh wasn't amused, but Violet cared very little about that. He had made this bed. Had he realized his betrothed was in love with another man when he'd married her? Had he realized the kind of creature she was? Did he love her? Or was he resigned to his fate? He certainly spent enough time away from her for Violet to feel a mere shred of empathy.

"We will both be coming along with Isolde, Tomas, and the baby," Father announced. "Perhaps you should set up a room away from your own, Violet. Ellie will hold her tongue in your home, but I can't promise there won't be imperious sniffs and asides."

Violet closed her eyes and asked herself just what she'd do for her family. Then she explained the events of Geoffrey's journey, Eleanor's story, his first father's response, the travel with Ginny, their affection for each other, and how they'd discovered a dead body. The earl replaced the receiver cursing, and Violet guessed that Geoffrey may never be allowed in their presence again.

Ending the call, she looked up and found James.

"Life is hard," she told him.

"It doesn't get easier," he told her dryly. He turned his book over on his knee and then poured her a cup of tea from the pot that was sitting next to him., indicating the place opposite.

"I feel like I'm pretending on knowing what to do."

James laughed with the same grin that Jack had, and Violet felt as though she was seeing her future in this man's face. "We all feel like that. If someone doesn't second-guess their qualifications at least upon occasion, we have to wonder if they're connected to reality at all."

Violet sipped her tea, wishing it were Turkish coffee. "Did you feel like you were talking into the wind when you tried to speak with Jack when he was in school?"

"Jack wasn't Ginny, darling Violet. It was a different time then. The war was on. We knew that Jack would end up serving. I was spending every moment with him, terrified that when he went away I'd never seen him again."

Violet's eyes welled in tears at the idea, and she had to take hold of her side. The sudden pain of a world without Jack was staggering in a way that she couldn't handle.

To change the subject she asked, "Did you find out anything worth knowing about the murder?"

"You know Jack already asked me," James told her, but he

was smiling as he said it. "I found out who the town elders are at the moment. I spoke with them about the rumors I'd heard about the donations and the village finances."

"And?"

"I had been putting out feelers already. Just before Ginny screamed, I was advised to keep my donations from Cowell."

Violet rubbed the back of her neck as she asked, "Do you think that was why he was killed?"

James's mouth twisted and he answered carefully. "I wouldn't find it surprising."

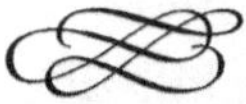

CHAPTER 14

When Violet entered the breakfast room after the telephone call, she was surprised it contained only Ham and surprised it contained Ham at all. His plate was empty, his coffee cup had just been refreshed, and he was reading a letter without a postmark. It was written on pink paper and Violet smiled at the sight of it. Ham looked up at the sound of Violet's next step and closed his letter slowly.

His close-cut beard hid the little twitches that gave Jack's expressions away, but Violet saw the grin in his gaze all the same. "Was this you?"

He gestured with the letter.

"A little bit me, a little bit Ginny."

Ham blinked, mouth slightly agape and repeated, "Ginny."

Violet snorted at this expression and told him seriously, "Ginny and Geoffrey fell in love through notes to each other, didn't you know?"

Ham took in a breath and held it. Ginny had given him

the doorway into Rita's heart, but Ginny was a schoolgirl. It took him a while to answer, but he said, "From the mouth of babes—"

"To God's ear," Violet said, pouring herself a half cup of coffee, sipping it quickly in sheer relief and then topping it off. Violet made herself a quick plate of ham and tomatoes and took a seat across from Ham. "I'm surprised you're here."

"Jack and I split the list of people we wanted to talk to. He had the vicar and the doctor, both of whom might disappear on calls. I had the town elders, who I bothered last night."

"And?" Violet lifted her brows, wondering if he'd answer.

"Jack hired Smith. He's still here. He says he's having Christmas with Beatrice, but he'll be willing to help out as long as it doesn't interfere with his plans for your maid."

Violet eyed him. "Are you sidetracking me?"

"Attempting to," Ham admitted. "I can't be the one who lets you get into this case, Violet. I love Jack more than myself and I'd murder him if he drew Rita in."

Violet fiddled with her wedding ring. It was just—surely, he knew what a challenge a statement like that was? She smirked at him lightly and he cursed.

"What have I done?"

"What indeed?" Violet asked him seriously. "How could you?"

"If I answer your questions will you let go of whatever it is that you think I dared you to do?"

Violet pressed her lips together to hide her smile, but the mischievous glint in her gaze must have been enough for him to realize that the independent woman in her didn't stay home when she was told to.

Violet took a bite of her tomato and then announced, "Don't you love hot houses?"

He closed his eyes.

"If I were fool enough to not just drink coffee, there's fresh orange juice. Isn't that lovely?"

Ham was cursing low and dark when Rita entered the room. The tension in the room notched up to full heat, and Violet fanned herself in the want between the two of them.

"Well now," Violet started.

"Shut up," Rita said, making herself a cup of tea and taking a seat next to Violet as though entirely unaffected by the tension between herself and Ham.

"Is this the magic of a few letters? Do we need to have the conversations we had with Lottie and Ginny?"

Rita met Violet's gaze and barely held back her laugh. Ham glanced between the two of them and repeated, "Lottie and Ginny?"

"Hmmm," Violet mused. "What do they have in common?"

Ham cursed, not wanting the answer, and then cursed again when Rita's father entered the room.

"Good morning everyone," he said cheerily.

Ham rose to leave. His gaze met Rita's at the doorway, full of wanting, love, and something of a plea.

He turned the plea to Violet, but she shook her head slightly. With another curse, Ham left the room.

"You two should be nicer to the boy."

"He's a full grown man, Father," Rita told him, rising to kiss his cheek and then make herself a plate of food. She loaded it with tomatoes, fruit, and toast and returned to Violet's side.

"You torment him," Frederick said. "Give him your hand or set him free, Rita darling. I love you more than life itself, but you hold a mean grudge."

"I was thinking I'd keep him," Rita said casually. "Though I may torture him a little longer just to be sure."

Her father glanced up at her, and their brilliantly blue gazes met. Their eyes were matched in that same awareness of how hard it was to risk loving after losing. Both of Frederick Russel's wives had been murdered. Who better than Rita's father to know about risking all for love? It didn't matter that Ham hadn't died, he'd pushed Rita away. She'd handed him her heart, and he'd rejected her. Or maybe himself. He'd assumed that because he was older than her, poorer than her, and less well-connected than her, he wasn't good enough for her.

Violet recalled those early days when she'd loved Jack and hadn't known how he felt about her. She hadn't been the one to open her mouth and declare her feelings first. She'd holed her love up in her heart, despite the pain of uncertainty, and he'd had the faith to speak.

What if she'd declared her heart and he'd refused? Violet was rubbing her side again and then announced, "We've visits to make, dear Rita. Eat up while I convey things that need to be conveyed, visit those that need to be visited, and gather up Ginny."

Rita stared at Violet and then glanced at her father as if to check that he was also confused. Violet winked and grinned and left them to it.

She dealt with Gerald and Geoffrey quickly, then stuck her head into Ginny's room and told her ward, "Dress warmly, grab some toast, darling. Adventures ahead."

Not waiting for Ginny to answer, Violet hurried to the bedroom opposite her own where Victor and Kate were staying. Violet knocked on the door and Victor opened it a few moments later. She heard retching and shook her head.

"Poor Kate."

Victor was white-faced with dark circles under his eyes.

"Do you need anything?"

"I daren't," Victor said, rubbing a head that clearly ached. "She'll smell it and it'll make it worse."

Vi held up a finger and ran into her room, digging until she found her aspirin and a glass that she filled with water.

Victor took them with fervent gratitude. She kissed his cheek and told him, "You might need to really consider something more than keeping track of cycles after this is over. There are ways."

"I've already talked to Poppy," Victor said hoarsely. "I never want to do this again, and it's just starting."

Violet patted his cheek and left him to his poor wife. When she reached the great hall, she found Hargreaves, who said, "Mr. Jack said you'd want an auto."

"I do."

"He said to tell you that he gave you a derringer for a reason."

"It's in my handbag."

"I would prefer to drive, Mrs. Vi."

Violet considered and knew that Jack would approve. "I don't know, Hargreaves. We're looking to be mischievous. Possibly we'll engage in hijinks."

His lips twitched and with a grave tone, he said, "I shall endeavor to dive in."

Violet clapped him on the arm. "Consider yourself conscripted."

"I would also like to be conscripted," Beatrice said from the doorway to the butler's pantry.

Violet shot her former maid a dark look. "I understand your beau has already been conscripted."

"If you need someone to break laws, tell lies, or step beyond hijinks," Beatrice muttered, "let alone find the crimes in a town full of angels, all the while looking like an angel himself, you've found your man."

Violet's brows lifted, and she glanced at Hargreaves.

"Mr. Smith is not charging you for finding Ginny."

"He's not?" Violet gasped.

"He's charging Beatrice. An hour of her time for every hour he gave her."

Violet's mouth dropped open and she said, "You don't have to do that."

"I—" Beatrice blushed brilliantly. Violet shook her head. Beatrice didn't want to be freed. Violet's proper, beautiful, honest, clever protégé had been captured.

Violet squeezed Beatrice's hand. "I'm the troublesome one between Jack and me. Rita is also trouble. I think my dear love, you're the anchor. That's what Jack is for me. He's the reason I don't lose myself, blow away, or dive too deeply into trouble."

"And I've found myself a pirate," Beatrice said.

"It sounds to me," Hargreaves told his niece, "that he found you."

"Took her," Violet murmured and repeated, "You don't have to do anything you don't want to do."

"He's not like that," Beatrice told them. "And I can take care of myself."

Violet bit down on her bottom lip and then nodded. "But you know you can count on me."

"I do," Beatrice agreed.

Violet decided that was good enough. There was a murderer afoot. Hargreaves brought the auto around while Rita and Ginny met them in the hall.

"Bea," Violet said, trying on the nickname. "I need you to pretend to be less clever than you are and dig through what you can find from any housekeeper they might have. The mayor probably has someone."

Beatrice blinked, glanced down at her nice dress, and said, "The housemaid should have something. I'll need a few minutes."

"Ginny," Violet asked the girl, "were Ruby and Rachel with you the entire time from the end of the play to when you found their father?"

Ginny nodded without hesitation and Violet nodded. "Then find out what you can without seeming like you're digging about who the girls think killed their father, if they suspect their mother—or I suppose their grandmother. Anyone else."

Ginny nodded without hesitation and Violet thought she might not be raising another meddler, she might be raising a female Smith. The sheer idea of it filled Violet with such horror that she had to swallow a curse and turn quickly away. But, now that she'd thought it, she couldn't let the idea go.

"Get what information you can," Violet told them as they walked to the auto. She held a basket full of food from the kitchens while Beatrice carried a box of generic Christmas gifts. A bottle of blackberry cordial, a pretty wool throw, several new books that Violet hadn't read yet, and yarn for Mrs. Oates's projects.

They each took a place in the auto and it was silent on the way to the house. When they reached the women, they found constables there already. Mrs. Oates cast Violet a dark look when she opened the door, leaning on her cane. "They suspect one of us. They're looking for the weapon that killed Max."

Violet met the woman's gaze. "That's normal."

"Normal? To think the wife killed the husband?"

"We're often murdered by those who have some measure of love for us. They have to rule you out. They search your home, don't find anything suspicious and then go about their way to continue to rule out other suspects."

Mrs. Oates frowned at them and Violet barreled in, taking control in the moment of weakness. "Beatrice, take the things to the kitchen, would you?"

Beatrice disappeared without directions. Better to get out of sight while Violet said, "I thought Ginny might brighten your Ruby and Rachel's day for a few moments. Are they with you in the parlor or upstairs?"

"The parlor," Mrs. Oates snapped.

"Perhaps a walk in the garden? Ginny might be able to help more than you know. She has lost family as well."

Mrs. Oates started to say no, but Violet simply stepped into the parlor. "Girls! My condolences." Violet ignored their shocked faces and kissed each of them. "Ginny has brought you some things."

Before their mother or grandmother could stop them, the three girls slipped outside. Violet glanced at Mrs. Oates and then crossed to Mrs. Cowell. Vi carefully said, "The death of a family member is a very difficult thing."

CHAPTER 15

Mrs. Cowell met Violet's gaze, noting the careful phrasing, and then she snorted. Her eyes were dry and showed no sign of crying.

"Who have you lost?"

"My mother," Violet told her. "My two brothers and most recently, my aunt who raised me after my mother died."

"And you?" The witty gaze turned to Rita.

Rita didn't hesitate. "My mother, my stepmother, my aunt. I only regret my mother. The worst has been my aunt, however, since I wanted her to die."

Mrs. Cowell snorted again and then she glanced at her mother, who had begun to knit again, her knitting needles clicking as she worked. "They get to the heart of the matter, don't they?" Mrs. Cowell turned back to Rita. "Why did you want your aunt to die?"

"She murdered my mother." Rita's head tilted and she added, "My stepmother too. When I realized what my aunt had done, all my love for her died. I helped get her arrested and then I waited outside of the prison when she was hanged. She wanted to tell me she was sorry, but I didn't want to hear it."

Violet had been there that day, and she reached out and took Rita's hand tightly. United, somehow, it was easier.

"What happened to your aunt?" Mrs. Cowell asked Violet.

"She was stabbed by my cousin for money that was left to me."

"Is the cousin dead too?"

Violet shook her head and said hoarsely, "She's in an asylum for mad women."

"Do you wish she was dead?" Mrs. Cowell demanded.

Violet's voice was a croak when she admitted, "Often."

Mrs. Cowell wrapped her dry handkerchief around her finger and twisted until the tips of her fingertips started to turn purple. "Then you know some measure of how I feel."

"Odd how you are both victims of murderers," Mrs. Oates said with a glance between them. "It feels like an unlikely fiction."

"I suppose that it does. Did you want me to swear it's true? It's more that murder brought us together. Our friendship was born in the aftermath."

"And now?"

"Well, our loves love each other like brothers. It'll be like being sisters-in-law."

"I hate my sisters-in-law," Mrs. Cowell said, flatly. "I wonder how long until they appear with their judgements."

"Why would they judge you?" Violet asked gently.

"I couldn't keep him satisfied. It's my fault he had so many lovers. If I had been a better wife, he wouldn't have had to do what he did."

"Cheat on you?"

Mrs. Cowell nodded and Rita didn't bother to hide her curse.

"That is ridiculous! They blame you? Of all the idiotic things. Men have been straying from their wives since there were husbands and wives and the lack, my dear friend, is because the men who do so have no honor."

Mrs. Oates nodded in agreement and Mrs. Cowell said evenly, "I do not disagree, my dear. It's just why they dislike me. Or what they use to justify why they dislike me."

"Were you avoiding his sisters after the play?" Rita asked innocently. "I saw you leave the room, and I'd avoid them if it were me."

"They weren't there," Mrs. Cowell said. Her eyes squeezed shut and her hands fisted. "I hated it when people fawned over him."

"We went to the ladies," Mrs. Oates said. "The one at the back of the building."

Mrs. Cowell flinched and then her gaze opened slowly. She met Violet's eyes and told her simply, "I didn't kill my husband. I wouldn't have."

"But you hated him?"

"Hated him. Loved him. I was afraid to leave him and potentially lose my girls, so I put a smile on my face and waited for them to be settled. My plan has been to move back in with Mother the moment Ruby and Rachel were standing on their own."

Violet heard the truth in Mrs. Cowell's voice and Vi dared to ask, "Did you care that he was cheating on you?"

"At first?" Mrs. Cowell looked at her hands. Finally a tear dropped. "I was destroyed. It was Leigh Black that destroyed me. She's seven years old, and she looks like a miniature Ruby only with different colored hair. I saw her when she was about six months old and knew my husband had a baby with another man's wife."

Violet could imagine it. Mrs. Cowell told the story with such carefully controlled emotions, but her tears hadn't stopped. It was as if the memory of that pain was worse than the loss of her husband now. Violet glanced at Mrs. Oates in silent question. It must have been so difficult to see her daughter suffer a philanderer.

"They never stop being your baby," Mrs. Oates said quietly. "Your children can have children. They can be independent. They can be caring for themselves and you, and you'll still be the mother, and you'll still hurt when they hurt."

Violet smiled. "Mrs. Oates, your daughter is lucky to have you. I can imagine how comforting it has been to have you during these times. I wonder," Violet said very carefully, "if I might ask you to use your wit on my behalf and help me with the names of Mr. Cowell's most recent lovers."

Mrs. Oates shook her head, but her daughter surprisingly said, "Yes. I will do that."

"Perhaps those like Dr. Black, who might have realized that they have a bonus child."

Mrs. Cowell closed her eyes. "Helene Black. Heather Sims. She comes and goes from his list. He's been trying for Elizabeth Lloyd but losing. I believe he has recently been tiring of Bernadette Lovell."

Violet wrote the names down in the notebook she'd taken from Ham the last time he'd bought a few. "What about the money?"

Mrs. Cowell paused and shook her head. "I have no idea. He never let me help with that. We have the bakery in town that I sometimes help with, but for the most part, I only manage the household funds and my own pin money. What there is of it."

"Have you had more lately?"

Mrs. Oates snorted and Violet glanced her way. "If my son-in-law was stealing or acting criminally, he wasn't doing it so that Shari could have more nice things. He was doing it for himself."

"If you had to guess who killed him," Rita said to Mrs. Cowell, "who is your guess?"

She just shook her head.

Rita turned to Mrs. Oates who also shook her head.

"Surely one of you has a guess."

"I won't throw out a name and ruin their lives," Mrs. Cowell said simply. "Constables are going through my things and your husband and his friend will be here soon. The only reason they're not here now is that they're going through my husband's office. I don't like being a suspect. I won't do it to someone else. I won't help in that."

GINNY FROWNED when she returned to the auto. "I didn't like that. I want to be a doctor."

"Why don't you like it?" Violet asked.

"Because I like them, and I was trying to trap them or someone they loved."

Rita rubbed the back of her neck as Beatrice got into the auto next to Hargreaves. "If my aunt had killed anyone other than my mother, I might have tried to hide what I knew. She killed again, Ginny darling. Killers can't go free because we like them. Or even love them."

"What if it were Jack or Ham?" Ginny demanded.

"I'd shut my mouth, look the other way, and live with the horror of who I was," Violet said instantly. "There is very little I wouldn't do for Jack. Given how well we know both Jack and Ham, we can be assured that if they are responsible for someone's death, the person needed to die."

"What did the housekeeper have to say?" Rita asked Beatrice. "Were you able to get her to talk?"

"They're stingy," Beatrice said. "I gave her twenty pounds, which was probably too much, but she answered every question I could think of."

"We have twenty pounds," Violet said simply. "It's fine if it was too much. What did you learn?"

"The woman's name is Jane Bush. She's worked for them since the Cowells married, and she called Mr. Cowell an avaricious whore."

Rita choked on a laugh and Violet had to admit she felt the same.

"Mrs. Cowell, Mrs. Oates, and both girls knew exactly what the mayor was. None of them were impressed with him, and all of them put a smile on their faces and pretended whenever he was home. Which—according to Jane—wasn't often."

"Does she have a theory on who might have killed him?"

"She said she'd thought about it a time or two. She did say something very disturbing."

"What was that?" Violet asked, almost expecting to hear that the man ate babies or took pleasure in destroying widows.

"She said he only seemed to become interested in a woman after she was married. Mrs. Lovell? He'd known her for her entire life, and he only flirted casually with her until she was married. She said the mayor took pleasure in taking things from people that felt like they were his. Being mayor from Mayor Potter. Wives from men who loved them. Money from those who didn't intend to give it. He liked to twist good things."

Violet gaped at the thought and Ginny muttered, "No wonder he was murdered."

"Ham once said," Rita told them, "that outside of abused wives and children who are murdered by their husbands and fathers, a lot of the people killed are murdered because they'd finally gone too far. It's why they start looking for motive. You don't just murder your neighbor. Your murder your thieving neighbor or your betraying business partner."

"What about my uncle?"

"The motive was money," Rita said flatly. "Money and someone who was probably hungry. Ham said Violet is good at figuring out who would kill someone because she's good at figuring out what makes people tick. It's the same for Jack, but he's also good at putting pieces of a puzzle together and following the evidence."

Violet leaned back and breathed in. "So what we've learned is that there are quite a few people who would have had a reason to kill the mayor. The problem with this case, like so many of the ones like this, is that so many people had reason to hate him, but who decided he'd gone too far? We need to tell Jack and Ham what we've learned." Violet considered for a moment and then said, "Hargreaves, leave me at the town hall and then take Ginny, Rita, and Beatrice home."

"No," Rita said at the same time as Beatrice who said, "I am supposed to be at the inn at 1:00 p.m. for luncheon. It's near to then anyway. I will walk over from town hall."

"Luncheon?" Rita asked.

Beatrice shrugged, and when Rita and Ginny glanced at Violet for an explanation, Vi only shook her head.

They left Beatrice at the inn, and then Hargreaves left Violet and Rita at the town hall while he took Ginny home before he returned for them.

"Is this what it is like?" Rita asked Violet as they walked up the steps of the town hall.

"What?" Violet asked rubbing her hands over her arms. The winter chill in the air seemed to have intensified to the point where Violet thought it might actually snow.

"Holidays when the man you love is working. You help to get it over faster?"

Violet grinned wickedly and admitted, "You meddle because they tell you not to and because they think they can order you about."

Rita started to shake her head and Violet snorted, hearing Mrs. Oates in her head. "Oh ho. You don't think Ham would tell you what to do? Well, he would. He did. He gave me the message, and I gathered you up and brought you along so we could send our own. We're meddling today because firstly, they wouldn't have been able to get that information from that family. And secondly, because Ham told us not to."

"So, spite?" Rita asked.

"Maybe a dash."

CHAPTER 16

Violet found the secretary at the desk and asked for the detectives from Scotland Yard. The man looked Violet and Rita over scathingly and then directed them to a corner office on the first floor. Violet tucked her head into the room and found a uniformed constable who recognized her and said, "He's in the conference room, ma'am. With the town elders. I will tell him that you came by."

Violet winked in answer, knowing he'd assume she wouldn't interrupt. Instead, she found the conference room and slid into the back, pulling Rita behind her. Several of the men looked up, stared at Jack and Ham, and then said nothing when they said nothing. The looks from the two who loved them weren't very nice, however, and Violet felt certain they deserved to be on Santa's naughty list for the way they were punishing her and Rita in their minds.

The man who had been speaking harrumphed, snuffled, wiped his nose on a well-used handkerchief, and after giving

Violet and Rita one more chance to leave, said, "Like I was saying—" he shot Violet and Rita a disgusted glance. "It's simple, Detective Barnes. None of us had any reason to kill the mayor."

Violet looked at the assembled elders, noting the former mayor in the room. Surely he had reason? He'd been so angry when they'd met in the pub. The question was burning on Violet's tongue, but she gritted her teeth instead, holding it back.

"But you do believe he was stealing from the village?" Ham asked with an exasperated expression.

The men glanced at each other, with one fixing his gaze on the table and another cursing under his breath.

"Are you protecting him or the village?" Jack asked. "Because I heard rumors about the money issues before I'd even reached my house. My father did as well. By Jove, Potter, you were the one who clued me in not to donate to Cowell. Out with it."

The former mayor shifted before he answered. "Jack, I—I don't feel right speaking ill of the dead."

"Potter," Jack said coolly, "do you feel right about helping a killer go free?"

The former mayor eyed Jack as if he'd found a snake in his wardrobe.

"Do you have evidence that Mayor Cowell was stealing from the village?" Jack demanded.

"The books are a mess," a much younger man said. He had a bit of squeak in his voice. "Secretary Coffing, sir. I've been trying to track things for the past few days at the request of the elders of the village, but the mayor got people to donate to specific causes. Unless we know how much was donated and what was entered into the books—it might be impossible to tell. The folks who gave that man money trusted him, and it seems he encouraged cash donations."

"Yes," Potter snapped. "Clearly, we thought that Cowell was up to something. We were investigating, but none of us would kill over that. We'd have had him arrested. People don't kill over things like this. Why would we? We could destroy him and watch him suffer all the while keeping our hands clean."

Violet's brows lifted. She believed him.

"We'll need the books," Jack told them. "If you can add a list of people who might have donated to any of Cowell's projects that would be helpful. Each of you check in with the constable and tell him where you were yesterday evening and who was with you."

"You still suspect us?" Potter sounded offended. "Well, I don't have some witness to my location." He avoided Jack's gaze and blushed as he blustered. "I guess you'll have to take me in. Of all the demmed fool things. Of all the wastes of time and effort."

Jack ignored the old man's grumbling and stepped into the hall to call the constable's name. When he returned, the men from the town council had left except for Potter.

He eyed Jack sideways. "Do you really think I killed him?"

"You made a good point," Jack told Potter flatly. "Why would you? He's been mayor how long?"

"About five years," Potter replied.

"Five years," Jack repeated without inflection. "Long enough to build up a good hate, but too long to have expected you to have murdered him. Perhaps if it were just after he won."

"He rubbed it in," Potter said in a way that challenged Jack to find some meaning in it. "He triumphed over me. He liked to call me the former mayor and then ask me how my empty days were going. When I started spending more time at the pub, he came and taunted me until he got bored with it."

Violet clenched her fingers into fists to hide her reaction. What a beast the dead man had been. She found that the more she learned about it, the less the blue days that might come bothered her. Why would her skies be endlessly grey when the world may well be improved?

"He sounds like he was a real piece of work," Jack told Potter. "He'd have tried to ruin things between Violet and me if she were a little less reliable."

Potter snorted. "She might have been beyond him, but he hadn't given up. He had a way of coming at a woman sideways when she didn't succumb to the usual approach. Perhaps you are right and your Violet wouldn't have given in. Or perhaps he'd have blackmailed her. Perhaps he'd have gotten her alone and taken her, making her feel like it was her fault. Perhaps he'd have persuaded her to a few too many drinks, but he tended to get what he wanted in the end."

Potter looked at Violet and noticed her white face, and then eyed Jack in shock. Her husband's feelings were carved into his expression. He'd have been the knight that came to life from stone to defend the princess. He'd have been the dragon who left the deep to find his maiden. He'd have been the monster that would have destroyed Cowell given enough time. Jack growled at Potter, took Violet's hand, and hauled her with him.

In the hall, Jack opened a door, shut it, opened another, shut it, rejecting three before he found a tiny office without window or occupants. The moment the door was shut behind her, he lifted her in his arms and shuddered. It wasn't fear. His fingers weren't digging into her back because he was afraid. He wasn't half-crushing her because he felt as though he'd almost lost her.

He was using her as the anchor this time. He clutched her to keep himself from going back to murder the former mayor and the town council. "He said that with authority."

"He did," Violet said, rubbing the back of his neck with her free hand.

"He has no doubt that Potter might have pushed a woman into something she didn't want and then manipulated her. Or maybe got her drunk and then— And he thought Cowell might do the same to you."

"He did think that," Violet agreed carefully. "Potter seems to think it was inevitable."

Jack finally dropped her to her feet and he shook his head as if shaking off a demon. "I—" He cursed low and darkly and then he brought Violet close again. Violet wrapped her arms around his waist, clutching him as he said, "I don't know why women love men when there are fellows like Potter and Cowell out there."

"Because," Violet said gently, "there are men like you, Victor, Denny, and Ham. Gerald. Even Geoffrey someday when he goes beyond this wart stage to something more."

"Vi." Jack pressed a kiss to her forehead. "I might murder someone if they ever hurt you like that, but I don't think I'd have to. I'd like to tell you it would never happen to you but that I'd love you no matter what, but I suspect the real issue would be that if it did happen you'd fight the man off, kill him, and we'd be burying a body in the woods. If it comes to it, and we're caught, it was me who did the deed. And I'd still love you."

Violet bit down on her bottom lip to hide the laugh since

he was serious. "I'm sure we would be excellent body-buriers."

"We'd excel at getting away with the crime," Jack agreed. "Precision is key. That and not panicking, I think."

Violet laughed and then asked, "Does anyone have an alibi?"

"Who doesn't?" Jack asked. "The wife and the mother-in-law were together. His daughters were with Ginny and Geoffrey. The men of the town council all claim they do, except Potter, but we'll check on it. Dr. Black has an alibi, as does his wife. They were together with one of the gents gathering money for the family whose home burned."

"What about that family?"

"I'd believe it of the father," Jack said, "but he didn't go to the play. He's staying with his brother, all their children stacked together like sardines in a can. He'll be all right in the end. He might hate the mayor—and he does—but none of that family were in the building, and they were together. No one saw them there either."

Violet sighed. "An excess of motives and an excess of alibis. What do you think?"

"I think someone is lying," Jack told Violet. "The only ones who admit they don't have an alibi are Potter, Mr. Lovell--whose wife has been linked to Cowell--and people who don't have motives."

Violet winced. "I had hoped the killer would be found quickly and we could dive back into our celebrations."

"Celebrate, Vi," Jack suggested. "Ham and I are more than capable of ending this case."

"But if we all work together," Violet told him, "then you and Ham will be home for more things."

"Vi." Jack kissed her forehead again and then she pushed

up and kissed him on the mouth. Their feelings rose up between them, and the kisses turned far more fervent than they should have given they had a killer to catch.

Violet took a deep breath in and then asked, "Is there anything we can do to figure out which of them is lying?"

"The murder weapon would be helpful," Jack told her. "The doctor said it was an odd one."

"It wasn't a knife?"

"Not a normal one," Jack said. "If we can find the weapon, we can find the killer, I think. It's long, slim, and pointy. Slimmer than you would think. The doctor is stumped, but he's working with the Scotland Yard men who have a little more experience with the odder weapons."

"Perhaps it was a prop," Violet suggested.

"They don't have any kind of inventory. Most of the props are lent from the players who take their things home."

"I wonder," Violet said, her mind searching for options. There wasn't anything she could think of. She felt like she could be looking at a table of weapons and wouldn't be able to find something like that. "Perhaps it's some sort of home-made item?"

"Like a shiv?" Jack asked and then kissed her on her forehead with a bit of a twist to his lips that said he was laughing at her.

CHAPTER 17

The next day, Violet and Rita alternated making gingerbread houses with Geoffrey and Ginny and singing carols to the twins while Victor and Kate collapsed. Sicking up the whole day long had left both Kate and Victor exhausted even though Victor had just held Kate's hair and rubbed her back.

When Violet and Rita were alone, Violet said, "It must be the former mayor. Maybe telling Jack and I how terrible he had been, and maybe knowing what he intended to do with me—"

"Wait," Rita said, shaking her head. "A man who hated Cowell claimed what the man was capable of. It might not be have been quite so bad as what Potter said. Potter also said that women shouldn't be allowed to vote because Cowell campaigned more to women and then he won."

Violet was rubbing her brow in thought when Agatha sniffled, large eyes filling with tears. Kate needed rest and their nanny was having her half-day, so Violet scooped up the baby from the sofa and twirled her. The tears fled, especially when Violet started singing.

Violet was in her fourth rendition of "I Want You for Christmas," which Agatha loved and made Vivi screw up her face and squawk every time, when the others finished the gingerbread houses. Denny had made a stack of decorated gingerbread rather than a house, ate them, placed his hand on his stomach and groaned. He hauled himself to his feet, pulled Lila after him, and whispered loudly in her ear about the romances of bulging stomachs and joint naps.

"Ginny," Geoffrey said, glancing tentatively at Violet. "Did you want to walk to the village and check on Rachel and Ruby? We could bring them some gingerbread men and escape before Violet gets Jingle Bells cemented into my head until Easter."

Ginny glanced at Violet, who nodded.

"How hard did you fight telling them no?" Rita asked as Violet stood and sang to baby Agatha again. The disdainful glance from Violet's namesake made everyone but Vivi laugh when Violet spun baby Agatha in a circle again.

"Not that long," Violet lied.

Rita snorted. "You hate it, don't you?"

"That they're in love?" Violet nodded. Of course she did. She barely knew what to do about her own love. How was she supposed to do anything but stumble through guiding Ginny? Violet cooed to Agatha and then told Rita, "It would be nice if you could just prop them on your hip, sing them songs, and that would be all there is to it. Even now, they have opinions. Look at Vivi over there hating my songs while Agatha loves them."

Rita shook her head and handed Violet Vivi too before she went for the bell and asked Hargreaves for mulled wine. The changing Christmas cocktails had added a fun flavor to the holidays, but only Gerald, Lottie, and Denny had been able to enjoy them without worry of other things that needed doing.

Just as Hargreaves returned with the mulled wine, there was a knock at the door and Hargreaves excused himself to answer it. He returned a moment later to say, "Lord Carlyle has arrived, Mrs. Vi."

"That's Lady Violet," Lady Eleanor said to Hargreaves, coming into the room and glancing around it with a sour expression. Her gaze landed on Rita, her scowl deepened, and then her gaze turned to Violet.

Vi lifted a brow, knowing the earl had scolded Lady Eleanor about how she behaved when she arrived.

"Happy Christmas, Violet," Lady Eleanor ground out.

Violet had to admit the look on Lady Eleanor's face was priceless as she fought her desire to once again comment on her slimness, her house, the way they were lazily lying about the parlor with—Violet had to admit—a rather excessive amount of cups for eggnog, wine glasses for mulled wine, and pretty cocktail glasses for Victor's creations. There were boxes of mostly eaten chocolates along with trays of sweets since the staff had yet to enter the parlor during the post-luncheon lazing about. Someone did need to clear the evidence of all their indulging.

Lady Eleanor's gaze lingered long on the mess and then returned to Violet. Normally, Violet would have cleared things herself, so it was an unusual sight. Babies, however, won out.

"Happy Christmas," Violet said lightly, glancing at Hargreaves. "Perhaps some mulled wine for everyone?"

The earl entered the room, completely disregarding the mess, and kissed Violet on the cheek. "I understand we've gotten ahead of our message that we were earlier than I had thought we'd be. Apologies, darling. I should have made certain you were aware."

"It's fine, Father."

The earl eyed baby Agatha, looked over to Rita and Vivi, and then he flopped into a chair with no desire to pick up either one.

"It'll only take a few minutes to finish getting your rooms ready," Vi continued.

She wasn't prepared for them mentally. Nor was Jack there and they'd planned he would be. It was always better to give Lady Eleanor that early vision of them together and united so she made fewer comments about how Violet could have done better.

Violet stepped into the great hall, saw her butler, and said, "Oh Hargreaves, do interrupt Victor from his writing"—nap--"and give him the good news." Make him come save me.

The doorbell rang again before Hargreaves had made it two steps, and he turned at once.

"That will be Isolde and Tomas," the earl said from the parlor. "Where is everyone?"

"James and Xxrita'sfather enjoy the library," Violet told him as she stepped back into the parlor with a bright smile. "Gerald and Lottie went for a drive, I think. Or perhaps a walk. They were debating over breakfast. Ah, Denny and Lila are in their rooms."

"Jack?" the earl asked. He knew that Violet had glossed over the one she'd normally have named first, and there was a little something in his voice that proclaimed he'd noticed.

"Helping out the locals with a little problem," Violet answered.

Lady Eleanor shot out, "Helping? What happened? Some woman get run down by a rogue auto? A sleighing attack? Jack the Ripper appeared?" She laughed as if she were only joking and then demanded, "What happened? Even Jack doesn't help for no reason."

"Father Christmas was stabbed in the back," Rita said dryly just as Tomas entered the door. Before Lady Eleanor could respond, Tomas crushed Violet in a hug as Rita took Agatha from her.

Violet squealed, ignoring her long-time friend for her sister. Isolde was curvier than before and in her arms was a small little fellow with big blue eyes.

"Isolde!" Violet crushed her sister, careful of the baby and then gasped as she stepped back. "Hello! Hello darling, hello! I have missed you!"

They whispered back and forth and then Violet kissed Tomas's cheek. A moment later, Victor arrived. He must have been shaken awake and cleaned up in a flash. Given his chin, he'd shaved, then changed his suit, combed his hair, and rushed down all while Violet had the defense of Isolde.

"Victor!" the earl said, shaking his hand.

"Where is Geoffrey?" Lady Eleanor asked imperiously.

"He went for a walk with Ginny." Violet sighed in relief as Hargreaves arrived with the steaming mulled wine goblets, followed by a housemaid with sandwiches. Vi would take whatever muting of Eleanor there would be when she realized that there really had been a murder and Violet really had let the precious son go walking.

"You let him leave?" Lady Eleanor hissed. Her eyes narrowed and her gaze promised vengeance.

Her father adjusted his seat, stating mildly, "He's not in prison, Ellie."

Violet took the baby from Isolde. Another distraction. She ignored her gaping stepmother and cooed down at little Tomas as Isolde whispered, "We're calling him TJ. Mother hates it."

Violet pressed her lips together to hide her grin. Independent Isolde was Violet's favorite version of her sister.

"Where is Jack?" Isolde whispered lower and then a little louder with, "Where's Kate?"

Violet's grin became a lie. "Jack is just helping the local constables with a project."

Tomas and Isolde's gazes met, their eyebrows lifted, and then Tomas asked, "Did someone die?"

"Father Christmas was stabbed," Rita said again with the same dry tone. "In the back."

Vi could hear the humor in Rita's tone, as could everyone else who didn't quite believe her.

"It's all true," Victor answered. "Kate is a bit under the weather. She'll be down later."

"Keep her away," Lady Eleanor said. "I have little desire to be feverish on Christmas day."

Everyone paused for a moment and then the earl cleared his throat. "Well. You're all joking about this stabbing, are you not? Didn't you get our note?"

"The local telegram boy was let go," Victor said with lifted brows. "He was found drunk on the job. Perhaps they're behind."

"He was?" Violet demanded. "He wasn't."

"He was," Victor said. "Denny was thinking of having a chat with the man who owns it."

Violet had to press her lips together to stop a curse but Tomas laughed uncomfortably.

"Ah well, now that I think of it," Tomas said, blushing slightly. "I believe I forgot to send the message."

"No matter," Violet told him, though he could see the truth in her face. She glanced towards the others and suggested, "Why don't we all have a catchup while Hargreaves ensures your things are brought to your rooms and everything is freshened. I know they've been working on it already, so it shouldn't take very long."

Lady Eleanor sighed heavily and then slapped a smile on her face when the earl cleared his throat. Her stepmother's eyes narrowed and with the earl leaned back, eyes closed, fingers steepled, she was free to shoot dark, furious looks at Violet.

This is your house, Violet told herself. This is your house and you don't have to indulge the woman. Violet met Lady Eleanor's gaze, lifted a brow, and smiled slightly. If Lady Eleanor were any less focused on pretending to be the perfect countess, the two of them might have already descended to hair-pulling.

"Lovely wine, darling," the earl told Violet, sitting up enough to take his glass in his hand again and sip. "How nice to have ham and butter sandwiches after a long motoring across the country."

"Thank you," she said, evenly. "I do hope the journey was comfortable."

The last bit had been solid lie. She really had wished they weren't there while knowing that Geoffrey needed the earl.

Her little brother needed one of those long walks where men said next-to-nothing but somehow came back happier than before. No one could do that for Geoffrey but the earl, though Victor, Gerald, Jack, and even Denny had taken their chances.

Isolde pressed her lips together to hide her laughter at the stifled silence.

Tomas broke it with, "Drizzly days, yes?"

Isolde's gaze widened as they were already to the weather and she bit down on her bottom lip to hold back in the giggles.

"I must admit I snoozed the whole way," their father replied. "Though I think I'll have a nap before dinner."

"When," Lady Eleanor asked shrilly, bursting free from her restraints as if a racehorse after the shot for the start of the race, "did you tell them to be home? The children of course. I cannot believe that they're out there, out there in the wild when Jack is working a case here! Violet! Violet, I am—"

Violet's father shifted again and even Violet shivered at the look he'd given his wife. She paled and Violet found herself replying to draw his attention for Lady Eleanor.

"I didn't give them a time to be home. They know they'll need to be back in time for supper."

"You didn't?" Lady Eleanor closed her eyes in real distress, but her tone was furious and it drew another clearing of the earl's throat.

Victor offered his father some water just to enjoy his reaction and because, like Violet, he was having a bit of sympathy for the demon woman as well.

Then they heard the clatter in the hall and everyone perked up, listening.

"Perhaps that's them?" Lady Eleanor asked and then shot

Tomas a silent order with her expression. He was to check and he rose to do so. The answer was, however, provided by the sound of girls' laughter. Violet noted the multiple layers of the girlish laughter and guessed that Ginny and Geoffrey had returned with the Cowell girls.

Odd, Vi thought, given their father was barely cold. She rose, handing back baby Tomas, and followed adult Tomas to the parlor door.

On the other side, Violet found the three girls and Geoffrey. He had been helping Rachel out of her coat while Ruby fluffed her hair in the mirror after removing her hat.

"Hullo," Ginny said with actual merriness. "We've just come to borrow a symphony record for Mrs. Cowell." She lowered her voice and whispered to Violet, "We've been trying to cheer her. She's just staring out the window. It's alarming. We left when they started arguing."

Violet would have replied that her husband had been murdered and this might all be in quite poor taste, but Lady Eleanor was listening and the girls were right there. Neither of them looked upset, and Violet suspected that there was a measure of relief with their father being dead. As horrible as that might be to say, Violet suspected few knew what a difficult man he was better than his family. If the girls needed to grab at a distraction and a little happiness, Violet didn't begrudge them.

"How kind," Violet said, taking the scarf that Geoffrey was starting to hang up. It was red and white stripes and quite lovely. "And what a lovely scarf, Ruby."

"Oh thank you. Grandmother made it, of course. She says she can't think if she isn't knitting."

"Geoffrey—" Violet started, but Lady Eleanor's imperious voice cut through the chatter and her brother closed his eyes.

"Geoffrey? Is that you? Come say hello, darling."

Geoffrey cursed. He knew it was his mother, so he didn't have to ask. His ears and cheeks were slowly turning an alarming shade of red as the feelings and rage he'd built up were coming to the forefront of his mind. He had been edgy since they returned, but Ginny had been distracting and cheering him. Without Ginny, Violet had little doubt that they'd have had sulking, silent, wartish Geoffrey on their hands.

"Isolde, Tomas, Victor, and Father are in there as well," Violet said quietly so Lady Eleanor couldn't hear.

"Father," Geoffrey repeated silently. His gaze moved to the parlor door and all concern for the girls with him was gone in his desire to believe that the earl really did love him.

Geoffrey shook his head and then glanced at Ruby and Rachel. "M'mother's arrived. I'll—"

"Hargreaves will take them home, Geoffrey. And Ginny can help them with the records. Perhaps, Ginny, you would like to bring them to your room for a girl chat and a bit of a private tea?"

Ginny nodded, taking the out from Lady Eleanor. "Come on, girls. We'll borrow dig through Violet's records and see if we can't find a few to lend your mother."

The last bit was for Violet. They'd been asked to take the girls out of the house if Violet had to guess. The poor women were probably discussing burial arrangements and how they would survive without the money from Cowell. She noticed at the mention of the mother, both of the girls paled. Things were not good at home.

"Go on with you," Violet said to the girls and then turned to Geoffrey.

He looked both furious and afraid. Violet winced for him.

He entered the room, crossed to his mother, kissed her cheek, and then nodded to his father. Isolde stood and kissed both his cheeks, squeezing him tight while Tomas clapped him on the back. Violet noticed Rita holding Agatha and Vivi, both of whom had big wide eyes that were a little shiny while Victor held Isolde's baby.

"Now that we've said hello," the earl said, "I wonder if we might use your parlor, Violet. Geoffrey, Ellie, and I are past due for a clearing of the air."

Vi nodded and everyone but the three fled the parlor. It was a bit of a traffic jam at the door with them bursting into the great hall to escape the suffocation tensions of the parlor.

Vi glanced back as she shut the door and noticed Geoffrey was pale except for the rings of brilliant red on his cheeks and ears. Lady Eleanor didn't look much better despite the even expression on her father's face. Violet flinched for them and then shut the door.

"Isolde?"

She shook her head, glancing at Tomas.

It was Tomas who said, "The earl's upset. That's all we can say for certain. I think even Lady Eleanor is worried about it."

Isolde glanced at Rita and then admitted, "There has been a lot of shouting between them. Mother—well—it can only be described as a tantrum."

"I don't care," Violet said flatly. "As long as Father looks after Geoffrey, it isn't my problem."

"Mother kept saying that a mother would do anything for her child. Every time Father yelled. A mother would do anything for her child. Anything at all."

"What?" Violet asked, shocked by a sudden idea. "What did she say?"

Isolde stared at Violet and then slowly answered, "A mother would do anything for a child. I don't disagree. Of course, the limits come when the 'anything' is ill-advised."

"Anything," Violet repeated with the most horrifying of realizations. "Anything at all."

CHAPTER 18

iolet stared at Isolde, mouth dropped open. She felt as though she'd been energized by an idea, and it wouldn't leave her be. She paced the great hall talking to herself.

"If," Violet said to herself, "the one had lied, then the other didn't have an alibi. Neither of them really."

"Oh ho," Victor said, moving out of Violet's way as she reached the end of the hall, spun on her heel, and paced the other way. Her mind was racing, and she was nibbling her thumb.

"If you take away the alibi, they'd have automatically been on the top of the list of suspects. It was only natural."

Isolde glanced at the others and then asked, "What is she talking about?"

"Oh my heavens," Violet breathed, closing her eyes. She left the hall and burst into the parlor.

"Violet!" the earl snapped. "What do you—"

Violet ignored him and turned to Geoffrey. "Did you hear what the disagreement between Mrs. Cowell and Mrs. Oates was?"

Geoffrey shook his head and then his head cocked. "Well, there was a bit about where one of them was. They were hissing back and forth and you couldn't hear anything other than little wails. Mrs. Cowell noticed us and told us to go for a walk."

"Did they say when the other was missing?"

Geoffrey slowly shook his head. Violet took his face between her hands, kissed his forehead, and told him, "You're brilliant, lovey."

"Is this necessary now?" Lady Eleanor demanded.

Violet blinked and then said, "I—I rather think it is, but—"

She was already moving to the parlor door where her friends were peeking, staring as she was putting the pieces together. Violet pushed past them and the door to the parlor shut once again.

"I don't want to be right," Violet announced painfully.

"The widow?" Rita guessed. Her eyes narrowed. "Perhaps. I'd have been tempted if that man were my husband."

Violet didn't answer. Her mind was on repeat. Nothing that a mother wouldn't do for her children. Vi closed her eyes and turned back to the hall, taking up her coat and cloche. Everyone was staring at her when she said to Hargreaves, "I'm afraid we'll have to delay in taking the Cowell girls back to their home. I need a ride to the police offices."

Hargreaves nodded, his gaze as interested in Violet's suspicions as everyone else, but he did as instructed without question.

"I'm coming," Rita said, taking her own coat and hat. "What did you realize? The wife? The mother-in-law? I could imagine it of either of them to be honest."

Violet pressed her fingers to her temples and admitted, "I very much want to be wrong, but it's all building in my head. Layer upon layer of reasons that make me feel certain I'm right."

"How will you convince whoever it is to confess?"

"I don't think we'll need to," Violet said quietly. "Jack said all we needed was the weapon."

"And what is it?"

It took Violet a long moment to answer because it was so ridiculous.

"Knitting needles."

"Knitting needles?" Victor gasped, shifting his shoulder. "Knitting needles—" His eyes glinted with gallows humor and he added, "I suppose it's in ill-taste to use that in one of our books."

"Victor!" Isolde scolded, but Violet needed that flash of humor to get her out the door and into the auto. It was in poor taste to murder a man with knitting needles. It was wrong to even joke about it. It was wrong to do it, and even if you would do anything for your child, Violet couldn't quite stand by and watch a woman get away with murdering her son-in-law and making scarves and sweaters for her grand-daughters with the same instrument.

JACK TOOK one look at Violet's face and nudged Ham, who turned and stared at the two women.

"They figured it out," Jack told Ham dryly.

Violet and Rita had covered their casual day dresses with wool coats, cloches on their heads. Violet had little doubt that her gaze was as wide and horrified as Rita's.

"Well," Ham asked equally dryly, entirely unsurprised to see them. "Who was it? All we've learned is that even when Smith is breaking into houses and using his criminally expensive eye to look over things that Cowell was, in fact, a thief and a blackguard. No one seems to have enough of a motive to have murdered him who doesn't also have a pretty strong alibi."

"Which we already knew—" Jack inserted.

"And now we're paying for," Ham muttered. "My superiors know who Smith is, so justifying him isn't exactly a walk in the park."

Violet studied both men. "Don't you want to know?"

"Not really," Ham said. "Jack and I were just discussing our instinct on it, and neither of us like it very much. We think we know. We'd rather we didn't."

"She's so nice," Violet said.

Ham nodded.

"She's not nice at all," Jack countered. "But she's witty, I like her, and I can understand why she finally had enough. Her daughter's alibi for her isn't wavering and no one else can counter it. We've been trying."

"We need the murder weapon," Ham added.

They hadn't realized what it was. If Violet didn't speak, they may not be able to pin it on Mrs. Oates, and she could go free. On the other hand, Violet thought, she would carry that with her. Knowing and not speaking?

She started to answer, but there was a knock on the door and Joan Oates entered. She saw the stricken look on

Violet's face and the hardening expressions on Jack and Ham's.

"I assumed you'd figure it out, but it seems that my crime is causing my daughter additional pain. I don't want that. I just wanted him to stop hurting her. So here I am," Joan said as though she were discussing the drizzly day. "I killed him. Stabbed him in the back. Watched him fall. I might have laughed, but I don't think I did. Then I slipped out the side door. It was several minutes after that someone found him. I guess that they were afraid to enter since he likes to preen and polish himself up, practice his smile in the mirror, all those things."

"Who did you want to protect?" Ham asked, but they all knew the answer.

"My daughter," Joan said. "I knew what he was, and I knew what he intended. For you," she glanced at Vi. "For Mrs. Lovell when he could catch her alone."

"Hadn't he already?" Violet asked. "I assumed that—" That they were already lovers, but Violet felt guilty for thinking it now that it seemed it might not be true.

"Oh no," Mrs. Oates shook her head. "Poor Mrs. Lovell was infatuated. Certainly she was. Max did have a way with words and flattery. But she is a good girl."

Ham sighed and told her. "I need you to write it all out and sign it. I'll need the murder weapon."

Mrs. Oates plunked her silver knitting needles down on the table. "My mother gave those to me. Always thought I'd give them to Ruby, but I doubt she'll want them now."

"I imagine not," Ham said, staring at them in shock.

Rita took Vi's hand and tugged her towards the door.

"We should go home," Rita said, sounding as if she'd rather not.

"I don't want to go home." Violet didn't see the need to pretend.

"Shall we catch the next boat to Norway?"

Vi laughed. "I was thinking I'd wait for Jack and then go home."

Rita laid her head on Violet's shoulder and they watched out the window as families came and went. It was cold and muddy with grey skies and a quickly setting sun, and that made the magic of those hurrying by all the more surreal. Bundled from the cold with rosy cheeks, smiles, and waved greetings, they had no idea that a grandmother was confessing to killing her daughter's husband to stop the cycle of pain and hollowness.

Violet could imagine the sight that would be happening in a few short days.

Children opening presents by the tree, lovers exchanging kisses under the mistletoe, and happiness that grew from an act of love and filled the hearts of families throughout the village.

In the Cowell home, however, children would be discovering just how much their grandmother loved them. Just what she would do for them, and they'd be struggling to absorb and carry the burden of her love. It would follow them for the rest of their lives just as the earl's love for Geoffrey would be weighed and questioned, which made those lucky children like Vivi and Agatha who would grow certain they were adored without the twist of a murder to taint it all the more precious.

Time passed quickly and Jack found them after he and Ham finished with Mrs. Oates.

"There's eggnog and a crackling fire at home," he told

them as though it would remove the gloom. "Large stuffed armchairs instead wooden seats. It's far more comfortable."

"But you and Ham are here," Rita said simply. "Eggnog and crackling fire. Or you two. It's an easy question to answer."

Jack and Violet left Rita to wait for Ham and stepped into the drizzle. The journey home would be better with her husband in the auto, their fingers tangled together, and they'd make it through the coming days easier and happier simply because of the presence of the other.

"Happy Christmas, darling," Violet said before they got out of the auto and entered the fray that had descended upon their home.

Jack's answer was a fervent kiss.

VIOLET ROSE EARLY Christmas morning at the sound, or rather the lack of sound. The silence was thicker somehow than noise. She went to the window and saw that the world had, in fact, been blanketed in quiet, muting snow.

She turned to tell Jack, but he was already sitting up. He followed her to the window, wrapping himself around her before the chill set in. They watched the snow drift down, admiring the perfect cleanliness of the world. Pristine and white. Renewed. Violet opened the window to reach out and grab a snowflake, when they heard the door below open.

Jack stiffened, but they both relaxed as they saw Ham.

"Ham?" Rita said from beyond their sight.

Violet looked up at Jack, and the two of them pressed up on their toes as if another inch would let them see better. It didn't. In unison, they leaned forward out the window, ignoring the snow as Ham took Rita's hand.

Violet bounced in excitement as Ham slowly turned Rita's hand over in his, marveling at the perfection of her palm in the way only a man in love could do.

"You know I love you." His voice carried to Violet and she silently thanked the heavens.

"I do," Rita replied. For the first time in a long time there was no edge of bitterness in her voice.

Violet silently gasped and held her breath, still bouncing as she waited.

Ham said, "You know I'm sorry I was too stupid to accept your love the first time you offered it. I can only plead stupidity and beg you to believe I'll never be so stupid again."

Rita didn't answer. Her head tilted as she examined Ham, who slowly dropped to his knee in the snow. Vi reached out and grabbed Jack's hand where he held her about the waist.

Ham studied his beloved, his gaze hot enough that it warmed Violet even from her vantage point. The tension between the two of her friends was blazing.

"Rita Russell, I love you more than I have words. Will you do me the honor of being my wife?"

Vi dug her fingers into Jack's flesh while she crossed the fingers of her other hand. She took a deep breath, held it, and prayed.

"Yes," Rita said simply.

They were all breathing heavily in relief, but Rita repeated her answer with growing joy. "Yes!"

"You forgive me?" Ham asked. "I need you to forgive me."

"Yes," Rita replied again. "I'm sorry it took so long. I forgive you."

"You love me?" he asked. He needed the words and the fact that he had to ask was devastating enough to have Rita make a wordless cry and Vi's chest tighten in sympathy.

In answer, Rita dropped to her knees and kissed him.

"Yes!" Violet cried and Jack's laughter broke through whatever romance was happening below. "Yes!" Vi repeated.

Both Ham and Rita looked up. Rita laughed while Ham shot Jack a clear command. A moment later, Violet was lifted from the window ledge. The glass was closed, the curtain drawn, and she was tossed onto the bed. Before her laughter could escape again, Jack followed her onto the bed and quite a different feeling overcame them both. Their early rising ended with a leisurely Christmas delay.

In the end, stockings were stuffed, rubies were given, mistletoe kisses were enjoyed, beef Wellington was served, the Christmas pudding was lit, but nothing mattered more than the love that was shared.

The END

Hullo friends! Happy Christmas! I am so grateful you dove in and read the latest Vi book. If you wouldn't mind, I would be so grateful for a review.

THE SEQUEL to this book is available for preorder now.

January 1926

Violet has received an obscure note, a strange request, and the claim of a murder. She'd like to ignore it, but the writer knows too much about her.

Has someone died? Who is the author of the note and why are they dragging Violet into this crime? Just what is going on and will Violet be able to reach the bottom of this madness?

Order your copy here.

If you're in the mood for a few more Christmas stories, check these ones out.

Christmas 1937

Georgette Dorothy Aaron has found her dream home, her dream village, and her dream husband. She and Charles are ready to dive into their holidays and create their own ideal traditions. When they're drawn into an unexpected mystery, they little expect what follows. Except for one thing, the reliable goodness of their friends and family.

Join Georgette and those she loves as they dive into the intrigue working around an excess of time next to the fire, milky tea, and Christmas treats.

Order your copy here.

December 1922

It's the first holiday away from home for the Wode sisters, and they're all homesick. All too soon, they realize they aren't the only ones who are restless.

It's time to discover why the dead are antsy, and what they're going to do about it. Will Ariadne, Circe, and Echo discover what is wrong? And will they be able to somehow solve the problem *and* fix their holiday spirits? Or, will they give up and go home?

Join the Wode as they rise up and embrace just who and what they are in this newest holiday historical mystery adventure.

Order your copy here.

December 1922

Hettie and Ro are fed up with everything. What's better than a trip to Prince Edward Island?

In between family obligations for Hettie, they discover a winter wonderland in Prince Edward Island. Oh! And a dead body.

Irritated that their retreat is blighted with murder, they aim to solve the murder so they can get back to their locomotive tour. As the conductor is the victim, they used their trip to search for the killer a board. But, Hettie and Ro discover much more than they expected. Will they find the killer? Or will, perhaps, the killer find *them?*

Order your copy here.

SNEAK PEEK OF BRIGHT YOUNG WITCHES & THE RESTLESS DEAD

APRIL 1922. WASHINGTON D.C. USA

ARIADNE EUDORA WISTERIA WODE

"Give me some of the good stuff," the man said, nudging a waiting girl aside. He was wearing a pinstriped evening suit with his hair pomaded back. Given the large ring on his pinky and the gold on his watch chain, Ariadne assumed he was quite wealthy or quite powerful or both. The large cigar hanging from his mouth suggested both.

Ariadne had been just behind him when he went shoving people about and she caught the girl he'd sent stumbling off her bar stool. The height of the girl's heels didn't help, but the man hadn't even noticed he'd knocked the woman down. The girl shot him a nasty, unnoticed look and then turned to Ariadne with a glance that said, *Can you believe this dirty bloke?*

"We're out," the barman said. "Want a Coke?"

The shelves behind him were nearly empty of bottles, unlike the bar itself, which was full. Ariadne sighed. The speakeasy never ordered enough, always ran low, and then the boss took it out on her. He needed either more suppliers, to quit under-ordering, or to open a little less often. Some of the fellows in the bar were reeling drunk and could have been cut off before they'd reached that state. Sloppy drunks put everyone at risk of getting pinched.

"Give me what the management is drinking," the man growled. "I know you got the good stuff, and I don't want any of this second-rate swill that'll leave me blind or dead."

"Our delivery of the good stuff is late," the barman said flatly. Whoever this shove-y man was, the barman was unimpressed. "No one's drinking much until that comes along. Not even the boss man."

Ariadne met the barman's gaze, and he jerked his head to the back. There was a triggerman guarding the door, and the man didn't move when Ariadne approached. His dark eyes fixed on hers, and there was threat in his stony expression.

Here we go again, Ariadne thought, ignoring his look and sliding past him without a flicker of a lash. Posturing was such a gent's move. She had too much to do for this nonsense. When she felt someone watching her, she glanced back and caught the gaze of a bloke with dark, sharp eyes and slicked back hair, with a hefty drink in front of him. He was, she thought, almost certainly a copper. Hopefully he was dirty. Otherwise, they'd all be hauled away with time in the slammer. The goons anyway. The shadows liked Ariadne.

Either way, she wished she was a little less memorable in the drop-waisted, shimmery dress that showed off far more of her chest than she'd prefer. She dressed with the intent to blend in with the other dames. Better to be seen as an easy moll than what she was—a lady-legger. Or, more accurately, a booze-making witch.

"It's about time," Blind Bobby growled as Ariadne appeared. "Do you have it? I don't pay full price for late goods. You're costing me a pile of lettuce, girl."

"They had checkpoints on the way in. I had to think quick and step even more quickly. You're lucky I'm here at all, and you'll be paying me the full amount or I'll take a walk down to the next juice joint. Easy peasy." She snapped her fingers. It was always better not to be too challenging, but sometimes she couldn't help herself.

Blind Bobby put his gun on the table and leaned back. "Maybe I'll just take the booze and pay you nothing, little girl."

"Did you find someone else who makes gin that won't blind you and can age wine and whisky with magic—because I don't think you have found anyone like me."

"I'll pay you eighty percent." He sniffed and growled, "From here on."

His dark, beady eyes fixed on her, and he leaned in, strong jaw gritted. He intended to scare her, but Ariadne was only irritated. She felt as though every time she interacted with this grunting beast, he thought he could just tower over her face and she'd crumple. Ariadne laughed, a trilling thing that didn't sound amused but conveyed her message.

Blind Billy nudged his gun once again, and Ariadne scowled at him, dropping all pretense of amusement. She crossed her arms over her chest and lifted a challenging brow instead. "Do you really want to put a *bean* shooter up against magic?"

"Do you really want to put you and your little sister

against my boys? There's even smaller witch brats in that town of yours. What's it called? Nighton? Bring her in." The last was said to one of the apes standing about grasping their guns trying to look intimidating.

There was a sound at the tunnel door and several men poured through with Ariadne's sister, Echo. She struggled in the grasp of…Ariadne's head cocked and gaze narrowed.

Lindsey Noel. She scowled at him. He was the shining son of Nighton and the fellow intent on finding his way into Ariadne's sister Circe's knickers.

"Well, if it isn't Lindsey Noel. Are you joining in on threatening my sisters? *All* of my sisters?"

Lindsey blushed, but his voice was mean. "I know where you live." His fingers dug into Echo's bicep.

"And I know where you live." Ariadne glanced at Echo, who seemed fine despite the white circles under Lindsey's pressing fingers. "Why'd you let them take you?"

"I wanted to see what Lindsey was up to. Sooner or later, Circe will see he's milquetoast playing at being a leading man. She believes that front he puts up, but the mannered handsome puppy will fade into what he really is—another arrogant rube with a rich daddy. It'll go easier if it's me telling her what he did, and after all—he put his hands on me."

Easier, Ariadne translated, than if Ari were the one who told Circe her lover put them all at risk with his playing at being a bad boy.

The idiot Lindsey let go of Echo, but it was too late. The smirk she shot him was enough to have him wondering, would he lose Circe over this? The unfortunate answer was that Ariadne could only wish.

The other men glanced at each other, smirking, when

Blind Billy grunted, "No one cares about your hick problems." He gestured and the goons lining the wall leveled their guns at Ariadne.

She sighed. "Until I get paid, you won't be able to open the bottles at the delivery point. Try as you might."

Blind Bobby laughed meanly and Ariadne yawned. He shoved the table back, grabbing his gun as he did, and shoved it into Ariadne's face, pressing it hard against her forehead.

"Careful," she said quietly, "guns do malfunction so easily."

"Open the whiskey, Petey," Blind Billy ordered.

Ariadne rolled her eyes and telepathically told her sister, *Draw your magic.* Ariadne opened her mind and senses to her own magic. She'd originally approached Blind Billy once prohibition went into effect because the church basement where the speakeasy was housed was a place of power. Her magic, always strong, thrummed through her with a vengeance here. Echo's must be a tsunami of power given the dead that even Ariadne could sense.

The ghosts are restless, Echo sent.

Of course they are, it's a desecrated church. How did Noel know about us?

Echo's mental snort seemed to ricochet about Ariadne's head and they both knew the answer: Circe. Soft, trusting, blind-with-love Circe. Lindsey Noel wasn't surprised in the least by their magic. Their sister hated keeping what they were from her 'sweet' Lindsey. She must have talked, and he'd gathered a full confession, given his presence.

Foolish girl.

The grunting of his man trying to open the bottle caught her attention. The goon was yanking at the stopper in the whiskey bottle, desperate to open it. He finally brought out a large knife, but it bounded off of the glass as though it were stone instead of a little bit of cork and glass. Finally he looked up at Blind Billy and shook his head.

Blind Billy pulled the gun back enough just to shove it back against her head again. "That's gonna leave a bruise." His laugh was ugly and he glanced at his men until they were snorting with unbelievable laughter as well.

"Balm of Gilead is an easy enough potion to make for someone like me," Ariadne told him, drawing her magic so deeply that her bobbed hair was slowly starting to rise around her face. "The bruise will be gone in minutes. I carry it in my handbag."

"What about the hole my bullet leaves?" He cocked his gun and then, to her horror, swung his arm wide, aiming at Echo. "Will it cure that?"

"Fool," Ariadne said, finished with this nonsense. She dropped to her knees, covering her head when the gun misfired, and magic rushed into Ariadne as the place of power energized her and she sent the rest of the guns into either misfiring or not firing at all.

With Echo there, ghosts were caught in the energy in the church and within the sisters. The ghosts went mad, merging into a tornado of shadows that sent Blind Billy's goons into shrieking like little girls. Point of fact, Ariadne thought as she started to crawl away from Blind Billy, her little sisters wouldn't have whined like these boys.

A moment later, the copper from earlier rushed the door. Ariadne dropped her magic immediately so it seemed that the screaming goons had gone crazy. On her knees, with forced tears, she looked like a victim as she reached for the copper. She screamed to draw his attention to her from Echo. "Help! Help me, please!"

Police swarmed the room, and Ariadne was yanked to her feet by the first copper to reach her. He glanced her over, muttered, "Fool doll," and shoved her behind him.

She shivered and whimpered and thanked the whole of the group repetitively with big crocodile tears, backing towards the wall. Her dress, her mussed makeup, and her tears were enough for the blokes to not realize she was one of the criminals. Just another doll caught up with the wrong man. She waited until they were all looking the other way, wrestling the goons down, and she slid into the shadows, pulling them around her.

The coppers didn't know about the escape tunnel where Echo had already disappeared, followed by Lindsey Noel. Echo had sealed it against any but Ariadne, so the fuzz were gathering up the men who couldn't use their tunnel while she slipped through, cloaked in darkness and magic.

Using the athamé in her handbag, Ariadne carved a rune of the door to keep it locked. She ignored the skittering of rats and the cool touch of the dead as she hurried down the tunnel.

"Go back to sleep," she murmured to the dead, hoping they'd comply. Otherwise the boys who worked for Blind Billy would find themselves chilled in body and spirit.

The old church had a crypt underneath, so it was better not to look into the dark entrances of side rooms if you wanted to avoid looking at the remnants of the living. The tunnels went from the crypt to beyond the graveyard behind the church, following beneath the road. Blind Billy's men had extended the tunnels even farther. With that kind of work ethic, what might those goons have been capable of if they bothered working for good?

Ariadne mocked herself—knowing she was a criminal too

—and moved quickly through the tunnels. There were exits for a good mile down the tunnel road if you knew where to look and what to look for.

The vast majority of Ariadne's booze delivery was still in the auto garage where one of the exits from the tunnels led. The bottles were loaded on the back of her truck. Echo already had their truck running and was just loading the last of the whiskey bottles that had been previously unloaded. Any speakeasy could make gin in their bathtub. Magically aged liqueurs, wines, and whiskey required a witch, a different country, or a very expensive operation that risked prison time. Ariadne sealed the tunnel behind her with the same rune she'd used before. Someone would have to find the runes she'd used and destroy them before the exit would open. Otherwise it would take hours for the spell to fade.

She looked away from her spell and eyed her sister. Echo looked a little mussed but none the worse for wear. "Anyone left here?"

"Just Timmy," Echo grunted as she grabbed the bag of their clothes from behind the truck's seat. "Poor boy. My spell got him hard in the gut when he tried to dodge. He'll have sore ribs if Blind Billy doesn't kill him for losing us and the booze."

"Did Lindsey get out?" Ariadne asked as she shimmied out of her evening gown. Echo tossed Ariadne a wool skirt and blouse, and they stripped down in the auto garage, changing from party clothes to one step away from an initiate for a nunnery.

"He got out when I did, but he was bright enough not to follow me here. We need to consider a change of employment. If things had gone differently, Circe would be raising Medea and Cassiopeia. I love Circe, but…"

Ariadne winced. It was true. If there had been more coppers or if the fellows were a little more trigger happy, they'd have been in trouble. With enough guns blazing, even witches wouldn't have survived.

Ariadne told Echo, "Aunt Beatrix said she was interested in taking over. She has more people. That…that…flimflam that just happened to us wouldn't have happened to her. Not with her sons. Jasper and Gerard with those broad shoulders and thick jaws? Let alone their magic? They won't get the same garbage we're getting."

"We'll still get our cut too," Echo reminded Ariadne with a telling glance. "Beatrix promised it when she wanted to take on the work. You engineered the spells for aging the booze like we do, and Beatrix knows it. We have to be careful, Ariadne—at least until Medea and Cassiopeia are older. They're too little to lose you too."

It wasn't Echo's words that convinced Ariadne. It was the memory of the gun being swung her sister's way. If Echo hadn't been prepared for someone to turn their gun on her, if her magic hadn't been inclined towards the dead, if they'd been firing guns haphazardly, if the sisters had been a little less lucky, Ariadne might have lost her sister. No amount of dough was worth that.

Order Your Copy Here.

THE VIOLET CARLYLE HISTORICAL MYSTERIES

Murder & the Heir

Murder at Kennington House

Murder at the Folly

A Merry Little Murder

New Year's Madness: A Short Story Anthology

Valentine's Madness: A Short Story Anthology

Murder Among the Roses

Murder in the Shallows

Gin & Murder

Obsidian Murder

Murder at the Ladies Club

Weddings Vows & Murder

A Jazzy Little Murder

Murder by Chocolate

A Friendly Little Murder

Murder by the Sea

Murder On All Hallows

Murder in the Shadows

A Jolly Little Murder

Hijinks & Murder (coming soon)

Love & Murder (coming soon)

THE HETTIE & RO ADVENTURES

co-written with Bettie Jane

Philanderers Gone

Adventurer Gone

Holiday Gone (coming soon)

Aeronaut Gone (coming soon)

Prankster Gone (coming soon)

THE POISON INK MURDER MYSTERIES

]Death By the Book

Death Witnessed

Death by Blackmail

Death Misconstrued

Deathly Ever After

Death in the Mirror

A Merry Little Death

Death Between the Pages

THE SECOND CHANCE DINER MYSTERIES

Spaghetti, Meatballs, & Murder

Cookies & Catastrophe

Poison & Pie

Double Mocha Murder

Cinnamon Rolls & Cyanide

Tea & Temptation

Donuts & Danger

Scones & Scandal

Lemonade & Loathing

Wedding Cake & Woe

Honeymoons & Honeydew

The Pumpkin Problem

Inconvenient Murder

Moonlight Murder

Bewitched Murder

Presidium Vignettes (with Rue Hallow)

Prague Murder

Paris Murder

Murder By Degrees